Advance

"To read *Flashbulb Memories* is to experience life's moments—both the ordinary and extraordinary—through the lens of wonder and awe. Saint-Denis is a gifted storyteller. A gem of a collection.

— Eva Lesko Natiello, *New York Times* bestselling author of *The Memory Box*

Flashbulb Memories

Short Stories on the
Roller Coaster of Parenthood and Family

Cécilia Saint-Denis

with illustrations by Stéphanie Weppelmann

Apprentice House Press
Loyola University Maryland

First Edition

Library of Congress Control Number: 2022950396

Hardcover ISBN: 978-1-62720-480-4
Paperback ISBN: 978-1-62720-481-1
Ebook ISBN: 978-1-62720-482-8

Design by Grace Noonan
Editorial Development by Claire Marino
Promotional Development by Shanley Honarvar

Published by Apprentice House Press

Apprentice
House Press
Loyola University Maryland

Loyola University Maryland
4501 N. Charles Street, Baltimore, MD 21210
410.617.5265
www.ApprenticeHouse.com
info@ApprenticeHouse.com

To all those whom life has put on this
strange and exceptional path of parenthood

"Être né quelque part
Pour celui qui est né
c'est toujours un hasard"
Maxime le Forestier

"Being born somewhere
For the one who was born
Is always pure coincidence"
Maxime le Forestier

Contents

Contents

Preface

As a parent, I have always been blown away by the unexpected, witty comments little ones can make. We watch these tiny human beings grow up, fly away and cease to belong to us. In fact, they never belonged to us, we walk part of our lives together, we just help each other grow. In our never stopping train of life, certain flicks or bumps take on an incredible significance, unexpectedly, or even disproportionately to the nature of the event. With time, everything around those snaps fades away, yet they remain ingrained in our memories, and in the family legacy.

I took the habit of scribbling down what felt like those moments in life to make sure they wouldn't evaporate. I didn't know what I would do with them but somehow felt like they deserved to be treasured and memorialized. Every single story in this collection is rooted in these snapshots. But, as they unfold, they often take off and drift towards an imaginary universe, highlighting the humor and the poetry that surround us without us realizing it.

This woman, this man, these children with whom we embark on this journey, both real and imaginary, are each of us. They are the children and teenagers in search of identity we once were. The constantly aspiring adults. The apprentice parents we become, more knowledgeable with time, yet never perfect. In the meanders of our collective memories reside vivid moments surrounded by clouded ones due to the passage of time. These are the real rites of passage. We do not always acknowledge them as such in the moment, yet those are the tiny sprinkles that sparkle our lives.

Prologue

"People have stars, but they aren't the same"

Antoine de Saint-Exupéry – Le Petit Prince

Métro Cité Universitaire
Paris, October 25th, 1994

Feeling buoyant and carefree, the young couple was holding hands and racing through the fetid metro corridors. As they got closer to the exit turnstiles, he let go of her hand to get his wallet out of his pocket and dropped it, scattering ID cards and used metro tickets to the ground. There was no way he'd find the ticket he'd just bought in the mess and they were already late for the movie.

"It's ok, I'll just jump, hold the doors for me."

As he was landing on the other side, he found himself face to face with a wall of ticket agents. *Where had they come from so fast?*

"It's my lucky day," he mumbled. "Officer, I just dropped my wallet. You saw me over there. The ticket for this trip is among these, but I don't know which one it is," he handed over a stack of used tickets. The agent, annoyed, checked all of them.

"None of these are valid."

"What do you mean? One of them must work, can you try again?"

Exasperated, the agent scanned all of them a second time without success. A bit aside from the interaction, she looked over towards the floor behind the turnstiles to see if by any chance a ticket was still there.

"ID please," stated the agent.

"Are you kidding me?"

Resigned, he handed over his passport. The agent flipped through it.

"You were born in Antibes? Where is that? That's not even in France."

"What do you mean it's not in France? Of course, it is. Besides, does it matter? This is a French passport. Are you here to inspect my status on the French territory or just to check that I have paid for my transportation?"

Shamefaced and arrogant, the transportation authority agent handed him the fine without further discussion. They left, hand in hand again, but the mood had been spoiled. Sure, out of laziness, he had not shaved for several days, which had the effect of enhancing his Mediterranean look, adding to his tanned complexion. The whole scene made him morose. He oscillated between indignation at the agent's discriminatory attitude and anger at himself.

"Antibes, not in France, seriously? Sometimes, such ignorance feels infuriating," he stated later that day. "I was born in Antibes. A flick in fate and I could have been born in Italy where my family came from, or Brazil where some of them immigrated." As she was listening to his ranting, she thought, that even though she was born in France, she could have opened her eyes to the world in Mexico where her mother came from or in the United States where her grandparents had immigrated in the seventies. When his tone calmed down, she added, "Where one is born is always a matter of chance." They would soon realize that, likewise, feeling at home in a place other than one's country of origin is, by all odds, the result of a series of fortuitous circumstances.

Westfield, New Jersey
October 25th, 2014

On a foggy weekday, the clan woke up early and jump started, as usual, with screams echoing throughout the house.

"She stole my leggings!"

"I have no more clean socks!"

"Are you seriously going to dig into the dirty clothes basket?"

"Why is there negative food in the fridge?"

"I swear I printed my essay last night, who took it from the printer?"

The litany went on and on. The phone rang. It was the scientist on her team at work who was not feeling well. While until that moment, everything seemed to be rolling smoothly, that call made the whole balanced system fall apart. She begged her husband to drop off the kids at daycare and school. It was her lucky day; he had no morning meetings and could sub for the task. She wolfed down a piece of a left-over pastry with coffee and ran out. She was always so fast in everything she did that it felt like her last words and recommendations were still inside the house after she shut the door. Her car was in the driveway, she jumped in, backed up and BANG! She had just slammed her van into her husband's car. He had parked behind her for no reason. He had never done that before. So often responsible for transporting her many children, she drove that clunky blue minivan. With the hysteria of that unanticipated morning rush, she didn't see his smaller Prius hybrid. Fortunately, there was no major damage. Well, none other than her husband proliferating some very loud words through the window before rushing out to move it to the side. She sped off to work and in what felt like no time at all was swerving into the parking lot.

She ran inside the building and didn't even stop to turn on her computer. She was pretty much up to date with emails, having read them on her phone as they were coming in since 6 a.m. In her department, an uninterrupted flow of volunteers would come in to assess newly developed beauty products. As she rushed in, she saw an early bird panelist already waiting. She took a deep breath, introduced herself and started asking the volunteer about the product she assumed had just been tried. Meanwhile, the technician in charge of the test's logistics walked into the room nonchalantly with a coffee.

But the technician realized the director was already interviewing the panelist herself. It took him a few seconds to put his thoughts together. *The lady has not tried the product since I haven't given it to her. The interview is supposed to take place after she tries the product.* He debated with himself on whether he should disrupt what was going on. Then decided to intrude with a question, asked his director if she could come out for a couple seconds and disclosed that the lady had not tried the product.

"Thank God, you interrupted me! I am losing my mind! I haven't done laundry in a week, there's no food in my house, I kind of crashed my husband's car. But you know what? I'm going to get myself a coffee too."

Having regained her senses after a sip of coffee and a few minutes of reflection that allowed her to reset her day on the right foot, she came back determined to leave her protagonist vest aside and shadow with trust the very well executed job her technician was performing. Panelists followed one another. Professional seriousness left room for a few giggles at times.

Taking things day by day was without a doubt the best life approach she could have, without forgetting to cherish every bliss, however small it may be.

Scandinavian Hotel, Göteborg
July 25th, 2009

The family of five, two inexperienced parents and three young girls, were on a road trip across Northern Europe. The radio was playing the latest Black-Eyed Peas hit and some Michael Jackson as the news of his death was covered over and over. Across the long stretches that separated Brussels from Paris, Hamburg from Brussels and Copenhagen from Hamburg, the family sang, fought, played license plate games and slept. In Goteborg, the sun had given way to clouds, but the thirst for discovery remained insatiable for these enthusiastic globe-trotters.

That night, after settling in at the hotel, she fell into a deep sleep, the day of driving weighing on her. She dreamed she was sipping a margarita while listening to a catchy marimba song on a warm Mexican plaza. The surroundings faded away… But just as fast as she had fallen asleep, she was up again. Was it the phone on the nightstand that was ringing? She grabbed the disruptive device and ran to the bathroom to avoid waking up everybody.

"Allô … Oui … Okay … Yes, I am on vacation … Great news … Thank you very much, let me talk to my husband and I will call you back in the next few hours."

The striking news nailed her to the toilet seat for a few minutes. Human Resources had just confirmed that her company was offering an expatriation for her family to New Jersey in the United States. Terms, salary and benefits were unreal. Everything was taken care of: visas for all, work permits, moving company, administrative procedures. As she slipped back into the bed, she digested just how shaken their peaceful every-day was about to be. They made eye contact and understood that some decisions were to be made. They had been willing to take that leap for quite a few years. Like many in their generation, they were always on the move, no longer aspiring to spend their whole life in the same village. The kids were still young. Spending a few years abroad and experiencing a new horizon and cultural framework was all they had ever dreamed of.

"It's now or never," he said enthusiastically.

"We always assumed your job would be the springboard for this. And now it turns out I'll be the one carrying the family on my shoulders, at least during the transition," she responded, expressing out loud her insecurities and the giant wave of conflicting ideas clashing in her head. "Work work work, so as not to put my higher education in the trash and manage the children," her voice was lower now, "sometimes it feels like trying to mix water and oil."

"Come on, you always tell me how proud your father was when he found out you were a girl and showed your mother the newspaper announcing that Polytechnique was finally open to women," he stated as if to remind her that gender equality was a given within their relationship. "I have no problem taking over the family logistics."

"Yeah yeah, I'm not sure how much your patience can endure." She struck back in closing.

They had always considered themselves to be a modern couple. Born in the seventies and raised by Baby Boomer parents in the context of growing equal rights and opportunities, both worked for big consumer goods corporations offering opportunities abroad. Despite the properties of the clay in which they were shaped, she couldn't help but cogitate all day on the turn of events. After sleeping on it, she decided she was not going to let herself be caught in the game of self-censorship and ordinary sexism. They were now in agreement. As everybody was still getting ready, she grabbed her phone and stepped out of the room. Two short rings and on the other side a voiced echoed. After briefly introducing herself she got to the heart of the matter: "I'm pleased to say my family and I have decided to seize the offer."

Château de Thiverval-Grignon
September 25th, 1992

That morning, from across the auditorium, she was the first one to notice him when he took the stage to campaign for election to the Student Bureau. As soon as she saw him, she felt captivated. *Was it the dressy light blue wool sweater he was wearing? Was it his overall pleasant look?* From far away she couldn't see details such as the color of his eyes or the shape of his hands, but he radiated self-confidence and inner strength. She sensed something intriguing and appealing.

A few days later, she bumped into him as she was entering the Student Bureau office. They had both been elected and were heading to their first meeting. This time, she noticed his deep blue eyes. They shivered in unison. They felt it, although it was hardly noticeable for anybody else. They grasped like a warm breath of air twirling around them. The first team get-together was short. Some members stayed and chatted a bit longer. Soon, as daylight was fading, only the two of them were left in the room. Draped in the growing darkness, bewitched by each other's voices, they talked and talked realizing how much they had in common.

They were both hungry for science, chemistry, biology, which they studied with passion. For him the fascination had emerged from the cradle. As a child he would conduct chemistry experiments in his parents' garage or in his Italian grandmother's kitchen. The ancestral recipes passed from one generation to the next by word of mouth made total sense for his practical mind. He knew the precise ingredient synergy needed to get the most flavored tomato sauce or a beyond compare gnocchi texture. In her, the interest had emerged later. During high school, she had oscillated between a fascination for the complexity of living organisms and an eagerness for reading and writing instilled by a captivating philosophy professor. She took the path of life sciences, feeling a job at the exit would be more tangible. Yet she kept a dormant appetite for writing, telling herself that one day maybe, she would do something about it.

On a more personal level, they also connected on the spot.

"I was seventeen when my parents decided to leave everything and go sail around the world," he shared. "My younger brother left with them. I stayed at my grandparent's and moved into college by myself. They live in French Guyana now. I can call them maybe every month, but it's expensive."

"My parents are divorced. My mom lives in Mexico. I've lived here in France with my dad since I was eleven. I also can only talk to her at best once a month," she said, as if echoing his words.

In their own way, they both had to dive into the deep end young, barely being able to doggie paddle. They felt as if they had found an unwavering shelter in each other. They didn't know it yet, but at that moment they started to fall in love.

Rue de Fontenay, Vincennes
June 25th, 1998

It was a bright summer morning, one of those that wraps you in warmth from the moment awareness arises. She woke up lazily and opened the windows to let the delicate invigorating breeze in. Her south-west facing apartment would take in the placid sun as the day progressed, shaking her drowsy senses and enlightening a day loaded with purpose. The morning street noises stirred up this energizing infusion like a magic potion. As she jumped into the lukewarm shower, she heard an unusual commotion coming from the kitchen where her coffee was brewing. The thundering noise took over from the usual hum of the coffee maker. In a panic, she turned off the water, wrapped herself in a towel and ran towards the source of the sound. Something in her felt sure that she was about to come face to face with an intruder.

The moment she entered the kitchen, she saw a mad pigeon flying in all directions, bumping into the cabinets and walls. The window was wide open, but in its despair, the bird couldn't find its way out. She grabbed a large tray and with wide but cautious gestures, tried to direct the creature towards the exit. Eventually, it found its way back to freedom. She closed the window and went on with her day after this freaky jump start. Fearing another intrusion, she decided she would stop opening that window. But her love for the morning fresh-ness soon took over once more. A few days later, she resumed her daily routine. To her greatest surprise, she discovered a splendid nest on the windowsill. It wasn't just a nest. There was an egg in it. She brushed it with her fingers. Barely touching it, she realized it was rougher than she would have imagined given the smooth appearance. Then, remembering that an egg should not be touched as the mother could then disown it, she pulled her hand away.

The next day, a second egg appeared. Soon enough, she saw the mother and followed her comings and goings. Was it the same who had trespassed earlier seeking an ideal place to nest? Soon, she realized that the mother seemed to neglect one of the eggs and it saddened her. Was it the one she had touched? She couldn't tell. One of the eggs hatched after a few weeks. She followed the miraculous birth of an ugly little living creature. The second ended up hatching despite the heartbreaking negligence of the mother. The mother fed them, until the first, then the other, set off to begin their Parisian pigeon lives. Until the end, the mother favored one among the offspring. She fed him more. It grew faster at the expense of the weakest who would only grab a few left-over crumbs. Nature played its course. The survival instinct would drive the mother to ensure the continuity of the species at all costs.

A few months later she told this story to her grandmother who presumed nature was sending her an unequivocal sign that it was time to start a family. Her grandmother's voice had always been her guide. She couldn't help but wonder whether she would be able to nourish everyone in her brood, whatever the weaknesses, whatever the challenges.

New Roots

The Move - 2009 and Hereafter

"For travelers, the stars are guides. For other people, they're nothing but tiny lights"

Antoine de Saint-Exupéry – Le Petit Prince

Fashionably Punctual

From the moment she accepted the move to the United States, she knew drastic changes would take place in her life. It was not just a logistical cataclysm. It was also a complete mind shift. For starters, she would need to drive, every day, everywhere, through any weather—snow, ice and all. Her Parisian life had not prepared her for that. In a country where cars were at the very center of existence and sidewalks a rare commodity, she would need to find ways to work out other than walking. How many steps had she taken throughout her Parisian life? Billions, no doubt. More than some made in a lifetime. In 1995, Paris had been the target of terrorist attacks. Since then, she got into the habit of minimizing use of public transportation and walking whenever she could. That would be the first major shift, a leap into the unknown. But then, she would also have to learn to be on time. While getting used to driving did not happen without a few crashes—luckily with no injuries nor major damages—being on time turned out to be more challenging. She had never been on time in her life. It was her biggest flaw.

When she was young, her father used to joke, "Everybody knows you are always late, so what's the point of even making an effort?" She took the precept literally and stopped trying. While in college, for her first date with the man who would later become her husband, she was an hour late with no excuse other than her poor time management. It was destiny's doing that he waited for her at all, considering that cell phones did not yet exist. The *Fontaine Saint Michel*, where they were to meet, had splashed some sort of magical dust, freezing time over his impatient, now spellbound soul.

Now, in the United States, her first meeting in the Manhattan headquarters was approaching. Her boss offered to drive from their New Jersey office. To be safe and to factor the traffic into their itinerary, they left at dawn, which was over two hours before the meeting.

"If we get there too early, we'll grab a coffee," he mentioned.

In her life, she had never arrived so early anywhere. They parked in a garage at the very heart of the theater district and started walking to their destination. As she trotted behind him, she saw a crammed crowd at the door of what seemed to be a theater. "What are you guys waiting for?" she inquired.

"Nicolas Cage is about to come out!" replied a woman with a breathless voice.

"Did you hear that?" she yelled at her boss, "Nicolas Cage is here and about to show up. Can we wait?"

He looked at her and without a word kept on walking. If she had been alone, she would have waited without carrying for the delay. But at that very moment, rather ashamed and feeling as if her teenybopper years were once and for all over, she gave up. This would be the beginning of a new era where her Latin origins, less stringent on the notion of time, would be brushed under the red carpet.

Turmoil

The move was approaching.

"Women who follow their husbands always put their job on hold. Of course, a guy knows his wife will take care of everything; the house, the packing, the logistics, the school, the kids' activities!" She started ranting, seeking support from her colleague, who was chewing in front of her and had just returned from a four-year position in China.

"I know, for them it's easy, they only need to focus on closing their projects and transitioning to their new job. When it's the other way around, it's another story. But it's our fault." The colleague answered once she was done swallowing, implying that shaking those clichés was their responsibility. "I have no problem delegating the most sensitive tasks at work, but delegating anything that impacts my kids, I just can't; but I should."

She couldn't agree more. Years before that, she cried for

24 hours straight before entrusting her daughter to a nanny for the first time. The mere idea of not picking out her outfits every day was painful. She learned to overcome the anxiety and moved along with her working mom routine. But what was at stake here was in a different dimension. The weeks that preceded the move were a tremendous undertaking, from the massive clean-up of the house, the administrative formalities, visas, utilities, moving company, up to myriad emails back and forth to ensure the kids were expected in school, dance and music classes. Since he had decided to quit his job and find a new one later, he had more time than her. They had agreed on who would do what, yet she couldn't help but keep an eye on everything. He was better at prioritizing whereas, for her, making sure the girls were signed up for dance lessons was the same priority as having WIFI upon arrival, which was the root of some conflicts.

The tears, the laughs and the endless hugging during the farewell party with friends, family and neighbors gave way to a horizon of infinite possibilities. The kids were ready to embrace this new life that their parents had painted with all the colors of the rainbow.

"I can't wait for our new house and for the big backyard!" One of them screamed the night before the D-Day. For their children, the whole move was also the promise of a new school and new friends. Yet crossing the Atlantic Ocean was a little scary. Leaving lifetime friends and grandparents behind wasn't easy despite the promise of daily Skype conversations. Not to mention the fact that diving into an unknown language was also a bit nerve racking. Once again, they were jumping into a new pool; and it was back to doggie paddling.

The movers parked in front of the house at dawn. He had

finished wrapping fragile electronics late the previous night. She had secured valuables and made sure no food was left anywhere. Her friend who had moved to India a couple years before had warned her. The movers are a steamroller. They work along each room packing everything they come across no matter what it is. And since the container may be stuck in customs for an indefinite amount of time, making sure no food was trapped in one of the boxes was of primary importance. She also remembered to get rid of all the toilet brushes. Another colleague had recounted her a memorable experience unwrapping a box labeled *bathroom items*. It was a fetid one.

The kids went to school, heavy hearted. It was their last day and they were ready for one last round of tears and goodbyes. By mid-morning, things were moving along despite the chaotic appearances. Boxes were piling up on the patio. By the time the kids came back from school, the entire house was inside a large container stationed along the sidewalk. At the end of the day, the sight of their entire belongings entrapped in a giant metal box, about to sail across the world, seemed surreal.

Unpacking

His mission that day was to receive their belongings while she was at work and the kids were in school. The trailer parked in front of the house. In a heartbeat, he found himself alone in a silent house filled with boxes and furniture. Everything had already been placed in their corresponding rooms. But the unpacking was no less than monumental. Not knowing where to start, he decided to open random boxes that had been placed in the foyer. Books emerged. Books, books and more books, of all sizes and shapes. Every new box he opened seemed to contain more of them. He was stunned by how many they owned; he didn't remember ever seeing some of them. The discoveries were all the more surprising that the packing of their belongings had been done by the moving company and they had not even taken the time to sort or declutter anything. He browsed through several. Started to read some passages. Raymond Queneau *Zazie dans le métro*, Gabriel Garcia Márquez *Amor en los tiempos del cólera.* There was something magical about unpacking things not seen for a long time. He had read some of these books years before the move.

When she got home, she bumped into an Everest of books. The children were playing hide and seek throughout the house, which, littered with boxes, offered an ideal ground for unique hiding places.

"Why did you unpack the books of all things?" She inquired in panic, floored by her husband's total lack of pragmatism.

"I had to start with something," he said rather satisfied.

"We don't even have bookshelves!" she continued, almost crying. "You could have started with the kitchen boxes. How are we going to eat, with our hands?"

"Calm down, I ordered pizza, the kids are ecstatic. Tomorrow will be another day," he said in the same calm tone. "By the way, the WIFI is set up. You can sit down and relax in front of the TV, which is also connected, thank you very much."

Kitchen towels ended up in a different drawer than the one she would have picked but everybody got used to it. She soon recognized harmony was reached without her being in control of all the chords.

Phonics

Their eyes were riveted on the Penn Station departure board, looking for the train that would take them to *Rahway*. After a few minutes, they gave up and looked for an agent.

"Could you please tell us which is the next train to Rahway?" They inquired.

The agent seemed puzzled. They had done their best to articulate, but they still felt that there was a good chance their pronunciation of the destination could be inaccurate. They had learned the hard way that finding the correct pronunciation of new words in English was often pure luck.

"Where'd you say you're going?" He asked.

"Rah-way." They repeated. Rolling once again the r and pronouncing a short [a] vowel like they would have done in French.

The agent raised his hand to scratch his forehead signaling a moment of reflection. His face lit up after a few seconds.

"Rooooow-wayyy!" He proclaimed pressing on each of the two syllables.

Over time they memorized the most common words and bumped less and less into new ones. They also became less self-conscious realizing that there was, after all, no right or wrong, since some words were pronounced differently in different regions, sometimes even within the same region. The trick was just to make themselves understood. Yet, some things would forever remain a mystery in the way language had evolved. What was the logic in driving on a parkway and parking on a driveway?

The Rabbit and the Turtle

"Dad, we read *The Hare and the Tortoise* in school today," his daughter stated with pride and a hint of malice.

"You read what?" responded her father, perplexed.

"*The Ha-re and the Tor-toi-se*," she enunciated, articulating exaggeratedly. "You know, *le Lièvre et la Tortue*, the same I had to memorize for school in France," she recounted.

"Ahhh, the rabbit and the turtle!" he exclaimed with the thickest French accent, the words resonating like a drum roll.

His daughter burst out laughing. It was a loud, deep, infectious laughter. The kind of unfettered childlike laugh that makes anyone forget life's troubles for a moment. No doubt, she was making fun of him, but he dove with his daughter in this outburst of joy and connivance until both wiped their tears of happiness in unison.

When they moved to the United States, he still benefited from a small advantage over his children. He was able to speak

English while they barely knew the colors and the days of the week. Of course, it was the kind of academic English that French people, who occasionally work with English-speaking countries, utilize. So, at times it was a little inaccurate. Nonetheless, he was able to manage and weather any storm despite his sharp French tonality. Feeling audacious at times, he would cram more sophisticated words, at least in his mind, like *hence* or *angst*, pulled straight from the old school thesaurus he remembered. Or he would insert French words like *déjà vu* or *camaraderie* realizing these could blend in now and then. The plasticity of his children's little brains, still in the prime of their development, led them to speak far better than him after just a few weeks. In terms of pronunciation, that difference was brutal. He resolved to live with it.

"Oh well," he thought, "the barista will never get my name right. I have no clue how to pronounce certain English names either." With that thought he pictured names like *Deirdre* or *Sean* that he would still avoid saying out loud. When he was in a cheerful mood, he would use unambiguous first names to avoid seeing his complex French name butchered on the cup. Often 'Steve' came to mind. At some point 'Steve' had almost become his second nature. He put up with the fact that changing countries meant swapping identities, becoming someone new. Anchors trusted from the cradle were shifted, new landmarks had become part of a broader landscape. He would now hear his children, who once hummed *Am, stram, gram, Pic et pic et colégram,* sing aloud *Eeny, meeny, miny, moe Catch a tiger by the toe.* Or *Girls go to college to get more knowledge; boys go to Jupiter to get more stupider* would replace *Garçon si j'enlève la cédille ça fait gar-con, gare aux cons, ma fille.* In his predominantly female house, the latter would be commonplace, with a similar idea despite the different lyrics. So-called cultural differences, even if they existed, would never erase certain human cross-cultural traits.

Punxsutawney

"Oh no, Phil saw his shadow." The young one declared.

Listening to her daughter, she realized she could never remember if the famous groundhog seeing his shadow meant winter was about to end or if there were six more weeks. Her kid's tone indicated the latter and, for once, she didn't look it up. She couldn't help questioning the veracity of this verdict though. Every year, just like in the renowned movie, the interminable ceremony was broadcast on television, chaired by a respectable looking individual wearing a frock coat. The whole event was watched by thousands of onlookers and remote viewers. Despite everything, she had a hard time trusting the odd meteorologist's decree given the surreal look of the affair. The weeks that followed were a succession of snowstorm after snowstorm shrouded in freezing temperatures. She reflected on the idea. Why not adopt the popular local belief after all? It was like awakening the child within her with a marvelous gaze on a world. But it was not easy to dethrone the Cartesian mindset in which she had been raised. While keeping her inherent rationality and her feet on the ground, she started coating her daily life with a touch of fantasy, indulging in seasonal house decorations, favoring certain colors in clothes based on holidays or celebrations.

Bumpy Journey

There is no doubt that she had fallen time and again since childhood. Always in a hurry, a tiny bit clumsy. One fall she still vividly remembered happened during her second pregnancy. She was two weeks away from her due date. Her belly was so big she couldn't see her feet. She was going down some crooked steps inside the hospital for her weekly blood work when she tripped. In an attempt to protect her baby, she landed sideways. A little vexed and hoping there would be no witnesses to her misfortune, she got up, scratched and bloody from head to toe along her left side. The distraught lab nurses rushed to put her under monitoring machines and luckily everything was fine. Memories of the scuffs and bruises would remain digitalized on the birth photos which were snapped a few days later.

Years later, another epic fall would be forever inscribed in the family memories. She was running along a paved and steep Parisian Street, pushing the stroller where her child was strapped. Maybe it was an unfortunate piece of gravel that knocked one of the wheels, or a larger hole between two paving stones. Without even realizing what had happened, she found herself lying on top of the stroller. The carrier was face down with her baby underneath. Panic seized her, thinking she had squashed her kid. Trembling and with tears in her eyes, she lifted the stroller. To her greatest relief, she discovered her little one, somewhat shaken and surprised, but not sporting the slightest scratch. She was holding her stuffed bunny in her mouth. She looked from every angle and realized that the silly stuffed animal had become a rather perfect airbag in this mishap.

Two dramatic falls later and she still hadn't learned from her mistakes, always wanting to fit more in her life than time allowed. This is how the fall of the century occurred after they landed in their new country. The one that would bring her to finally slow down. As she was running around her car, for some unknown reason which could be none other than the fact that she was always running, she stumbled and fell face flat on the concrete floor. Her husband, who was waiting in the car and witnessed the scene from the rear-view mirror, rushed towards her.

"Don't panic, but I'm just warning you that there is a huge chicken egg growing on your forehead," he said in a tone that was half reassuring and half concerning. After rushing to the closest Urgent Care, where they spent more time filling out paperwork than seeing a doctor, she dedicated the rest of her day to applying successive ice patches in the hopes of reducing the deformity that would settle and remain on her face for an indefinite duration. Even so, the next day, she woke up with a monstrous, swollen black eye that no makeup and no sun-glasses would ever be able to hide. She gave herself a push, muscled up her courage and went on with her day, ready to tell her pathetic little story to the entire world. A few days later, as she was returning to her car after dropping her daughter off at the daycare, a woman approached her in the parking lot.

"Hi… I'm sorry to bother you. I've been meaning to talk to you for a few days. I was unsure but…" She mumbled with obvious hesitation. "I'm a lawyer, you know and my husband is a police officer. I know you are here in this country alone. So, if you ever need help…" She continued. Her determination seemed to strengthen a little.

For her part, she was so absorbed in the worries of her daily life that she had forgotten that she was walking around with a hideous protuberance on her face. She stared at the woman dazed and confused. Lawyer, police, help, alone. What was she talking about? Until the juxtaposition of random words took an eye-opening turn. Her face lit up.

"I appreciate you coming to me. I'm not the victim of any kind of abuse. I just faceplanted on the asphalt," she said.

As the woman was getting into her car, just half convinced, she stood there for a while, wondering about the number of women in the world who needed such a lifesaver and did not have it. In retrospect, her falls were nothing compared to some others' misfortune.

Chaperones

Some say that when you have children you don't choose your friends anymore, they choose them for you. Perhaps this is a blessing in disguise. Most of the time they select more wisely than adults. They follow their instincts and their hearts without preconceptions or mental barriers.

That fateful day she decided to take off from work in order to chaperone one of her children's field trips. Chaperoning a class trip seemed to be something within reach for her. How different could it be from one country to another? A bus with very loud children on the way out and run-down sleepy children on the way back, a teacher counting children before getting on the bus, once on the bus, when getting out of the bus, when getting back on the bus... For some reason, she liked being called a *chaperone*. She found the word ancient in a nice way. It evoked courting on a Victorian porch in a Jane Austen novel and those Victorian homes that flourished on the East

Coast that fascinated her.

"I heard you moved from France in the beginning of this school year," said this other mom in an engaging tone. And there, she met one of her future dearest friends, another chaperone, who happened to be the mother of a little girl who had been her daughter's best friend from day one. The friendship solidified and they soon started planning family get togethers. Other lifelong friends were met at a dance studio or along a Halloween trick or treat walk, always initiated by the children. These child-motivated encounters always led to higher compatibility than the ones they attempted as adults. How many times had they tried to forge relationships colliding with a void, a lack of conversation topics, or incompatible values? Yet, when engaging conversations with adults introduced to them by their children, talks would always deviate from the original fundraiser or sport encounter onto more personal matters, as if by magic their thoughts processes and views were similar. It was as if the children, rather than the adults, were the chaperones on the path towards adjustment.

Cultural Differences

The children adapted faster than the parents would have imagined. For a long time, they wondered how they would explain that it would no longer be a French little mouse but an American fairy who would swap their tooth for a coin in the middle of the night, or that it would no longer be flying bells that would throw chocolate eggs from the sky on Easter but little bunnies dropping them instead.

One morning, as she had forgotten for the third night in a row that a tooth was awaiting under one of the pillows, her daughter knocked on the bathroom door.

"Just give me the money and let's be over with this!" she ordered.

She objected, shocked by her daughter's nerve. She was also filled with relief, realizing that the questions that had been haunting them as parents would not even be relevant for the older ones. To their surprise, the youngest, still gullible, didn't question the new origin of the treats either. They wondered if their adaptability had led them to embody the precept *When in Rome, do as Romans do*. Or else their mischievousness was such that the messenger, who they never met, did not matter, as long as the gifts were there.

Working vs.
Stay-at-Home Mom

They were now acclimated to the busy American way of life. This meant that it always came as a relief when May would show the tip of its nose and announce the summer months, warmer days, lighter clothes, tanned skin and most importantly: summer hours. Employees who agreed to work one extra hour Monday through Thursday, had their Friday afternoons off. Living in New Jersey, summer was synonymous with weekends down the shore for most. That was just a fact. Most companies would allow their employees to hit the road before intense traffic. They, meanwhile, were not hard-core beachgoers. Even so, her greatest joy of the week was being able to go home, eat a big plate of pasta with butter in front of the TV and pick up the kids at school. As a working mom, not to be the last parent at the daycare for once and to be at the school door for dismissal to experience the fever of the outburst of kids, were dreams long unfulfilled. Exchanging a few words with the teacher, witnessing the last goodbyes and Lego swaps, listening to the fresh anecdotes which would later be forgotten or picking up a sweater loosely wrapped around the backpack strap were all just simple joys she would live to the full.

"Can we have a playdate with Thomas?"

"Yes!"

"The ice cream truck! Can we get ice cream?"

"Why not!"

Everything she could do to brush off her working mom guilt would be a ten thousand times yes. Too often her kids would tell her at night how after school their friend's mom would have baked cookies waiting at home. While listening and envisioning the smell and the happy faces, she pictured herself at that time in a meeting discussing shampoo launches. Without a doubt more lucrative and the reason why she was balancing everything. But what was the true meaning of her existence? What would she remember when looking back ten or twenty years from now?

The rest of the week was a juggle, arranging carpools for her kids to get where they needed to be in exchange for her driving everybody home at night. Business trips were torture with both the logistics to put into place and the emotional tear that it represented. Sometimes she would cry inconsolably the day before, when the trip involved international flying for a week or more. People would often comment: "I don't know how you do it!" Her inner response was always "I don't know how I do it. I fight entropy on a daily basis and it comes with tradeoffs." But one thing was sure; she worked hard to renounce perfection, delegate, be able to say no and make the best use of her time.

Social Breakthrough

She never understood if it was because she was from else-where or if it was the fact that she never quite fit into the world of stay-at-home moms *or* working moms, but building bonds with moms at school was not her strong suit. Trivial "hellos" and "how are yous?" were usually the farthest she ventured, trying to find her way amidst groups that seemed like they had known each other forever. She couldn't help but wonder if it was just her feeling like an outcast at times, or if maybe each parent entering the school grounds felt the same and pre-tended to be at ease.

Good Eye

All the parents share universal experiences: attending a concert when your child plays an instrument, sings in a choir or dances in a recital. Without exception, parents know what to expect. They know what time it starts, what time it ends. Mothers know that they will shed a tear at the sight of their child. Both parents know they have to be patient with instrumental hiccups or uncoordinated choreography that may be painful to hear or watch. Every parent ends the night proud of their kid who always stands out among all in their eyes. Sport meets and games also unfold similarly no matter where the parents may be. A track meet forces them to get up early, drive to the end of the world, separate from their child upon arrival and spend the day wondering where and when they will be running. The parent may catch a glimpse of the run, just enough for a brief shout out and a blurry action shot, or they may downright miss their kid because the long-awaited race ends up taking place right when they decide to go get food to survive.

When their daughters decided to try softball, they thought they knew what they were getting themselves into, without realizing the scene would be set for them to deep dive into the American life. First, they had to acquire the equipment, which proved to be more complicated than getting last minute school supplies at the start of a new school year. Figuring out what a *marble notebook* was and finding it had been a quest, but rather easy compared to diving into the technicality and sizes of the different mits, helmets, cleats and bats. They were told the glove had to be broken in. They had no idea what that meant or how to do it. Later on, came practices and games. Parents at the edge of the field seemed invested to the highest degree. The jargon flew over their heads, confused and ignorant of the rules as they were. It didn't take too long for them to understand what an *inning* or a *home run* was. But they were rather unclear on how long the inning was supposed to be, how many there were total, how long the whole game was supposed to last. The rules also seemed to vary with age and leagues. Why was the batter not even trying to hit the ball sometimes? They realized it had to hit a certain abstract target. This imaginary window within which the ball was to go through for everybody to shout "strike!" left them flat out perplexed. How far down was the rectangle supposed to stretch out? It seemed subjective and based on the appreciation of a few connoisseurs. In the middle of all those words thrown in the air, she kept hearing one particular two-syllable sound. In her mind, she understood it as "goudy." It was spewed by onlookers just after the pitcher threw the ball towards the batter. She told herself that it had to be another technical word to describe the throw. The tone always sounded encouraging rather than negative. She also noticed the word seemed to be uttered when the batter was not swinging the bat. It was only after several weeks of silent observation, research and deduction, that the epiphany came. Maybe it was someone's intonation that triggered it. It wasn't one word; it was two separate words. "Good eye," meaning that the batter had noticed that the ball was not in that phantasmagoric strike zone. Out of the blue, everything made sense. From that moment on, she felt that she belonged at last.

A few years later, when their youngest son reached age, they thought that it was their duty to make him try the national sport that they now knew a little better. Far be it from them to say they knew it all though. Once his first season was over, he expressed that the whole thing had been rather boring. Soccer, where a lot more was going on, according to him, was his preference without hesitation. The parents, proud of the Italian, French and Mexican blood flowing through their veins, couldn't conceal how fulfilled they felt by their little one's verdict. They would be able to cheer knowingly and confidently for years to come.

Good Job

Their child, freshly immersed in an American 2nd grade, came back from school that day with all the multiplication facts on a sheet.

"We have to learn these for tomorrow," she stated.

"You have to know all the multiplication tables for tomorrow?" said the mother in disbelief, remembering how painful it had been for her oldest to memorize them and how several school years had been spent doing that.

"Well, the teacher said to go over them, not to know them," responded the little voice, "I'm done by the way, can I go play?"

The next day, the mother decided to go see the teacher.

"I wanted to ask you, what do you expect from the kids for the multiplication facts? Do they have to memorize all of them at once?" she asked. Her tone hinted a slight panic.

"Of course not, I just want them to familiarize with them.

They are going to go over them in third, fourth and fifth grade. Don't worry," answered the teacher.

A few years later, the parents realized that the tables had been memorized, infused in the brain somehow. The whole process had been less painful than the French way where they were learned the hard way, the old-fashioned way, hammered in their head.

They had been told that mathematics was taught differently. They were now experiencing that in the flesh. The dad had an epiphany one day when he realized that a fundamental difference at the very heart of the approach was in the terminology. Unlike in France, in elementary school, kids were not exposed to *problems*, but to *stories with numbers*.

"It may not look like much of a difference," he thought, "but at the end of the day, it translates into a bluntly different mindset. In these kids' brains, life is not a universe full of complications, but a magic world populated by numbers."

They also soon understood that the stories' themes more often than not revolved around money and distribution of goods. Learning how to count in nickel, dime or quarter units, was more pragmatic to train future consumers than knowing how long it would take to fill a bucket based on water flow. For the parents, talking money also meant avoiding dealing with weights, volumes and temperatures in the imperial system which was always a good thing.

Little by little they got used to the learning differences and even embraced many of them. They also adjusted to small dissimilarities in everyday life. Their children's lunch boxes, exuberant for some at first, began to look more like those of their classmates. Even though their children preferred ratatouille in a thermos over a plain ham sandwich, at certain ages the peer pressure was stronger than anything.

But sometimes, the parents could just not stop their true colors from shining true. One day, one of the girls came home and exhibited her math test with a magnificent *Good Job* written on the top in red. The mother started turning the pages noting that not everything was correct and the presentation was careless, almost unreadable.

"Why did she write *Good Job*? You made mistakes and it's so sloppy," said the mother in a very French never-good-enough tone.

"You are so mean, I was so happy. You always ruin everything," said the child, running over to her room and locking the door.

And at that moment, the parents realized that they would have to strike a proper balance between the French way of pointing out what is *Not Good Enough* and the American unconditional *Good Job* approach, between the French *NO, don't do that!* and the American positive reinforcement *Hey why don't we make cookies*, while the kid is about to draw with permanent markers on the wall. As their children grew up strengthened by their dual cultural affiliation and able to see life from different lenses, they too became more adaptable and aware that in a cultural clash, not all is black on one side and white on the other, but that there is common ground to be found.

Timeless September

Each year, September came faster than expected. Sometimes it even felt as if the entire year had been an ethereal shooting star sandwiched between two Septembers. She became almost persuaded that the very reason for this month's existence was to test her organizational skills as a working mother. The girls were now older and each signed up for multiple dance classes, music lessons, acting, sewing, track … Putting together the family schedule had been an impossible puzzle. Now kids were back to school, first week, she was going to be put to the test. But she felt ready, she had even printed multiple copies of the schedule for the nanny, for her car, for him (although he never read it and even by June had only a vague idea of it). That day at work had been draining: morning meeting, lunch meeting, post lunch meeting, hundreds of emails, team issues to be resolved. At the end of the day somehow, even if she had not done half of what she intended to, she felt accomplished and liberated as she jumped into her car to head back home. She opened the front door and at the very moment that her eyes met the nanny's, it was as if a lightning had struck her. She had just realized what she was going to hear. She had forgotten to pick up her daughter from dance. She jumped into the car. As she entered the lobby of the dance studio, she saw her waiting, chatting with one of the teachers. A deep sensation of guilt was already rising inside her throat when her daughter threw herself at her and said:

"With all the things that you were likely to forget, it is me that you forgot."

Recurring September

She woke up in sweats, dreams and reality still intertwined in her mind. She now knew she was dreaming, no, not dreaming, having the worst nightmare. She was still pretty shaken. In the middle of her peaceful slumber, all of a sudden, it was Halloween and she didn't have any costumes. She knew it was unthinkable to use the same costumes as the year before. The classic type of nightmare a mother of several kids, each in a different school, could have during the month of September. Let's say, to be more precise, for an American mother, or for a French mother getting used to the American customs. Apart from that, September was always a strange mix of emotions and anxiety. Back to school involved hundreds of school forms, shopping, waking up from the unruled routine of summer days. One year in particular, for the first time, she resolved to not do things last minute. In early August, she printed out all the forms, went ahead and filled out everything: contact information for pediatrician, dentist, eye doctor, dates of last check-ups, vaccines, insurance and so on and so forth. She felt proud and accomplished. On the first day of school, she discovered, horrified that she had to start all over again on a brand-new online platform. The one year she had gotten ahead had been the year the school district had decided to carry out the transition from paper to online. So much for being ahead of the game! On the phone, the nurse told her that she could file her paper forms just this time. But she decided to bow down to modernity, knowing full well that if it was not now, she would have to do it at some point. Yes, modernity had its advantages: from now on only minor updates to every form would be required.

September was not entirely unpleasant though. Schedules fell back into a certain order of things as opposed to the anarchy of summer. For older kids, late nights were only allowed on Fridays or Saturdays; for her that meant more peaceful sleep during the week.

Extreme Coupon Lady

She was standing in line at the grocery store that morning. She had been aware for several days that there would soon be no more diapers in her child's cubby. The day before, they had run out. And the stock at home had vanished as well, which she remembered as she woke up in the morning. Therefore, she was forced to stop by the store before dropping her baby off at daycare and rushing off to work.

The lady's cart in front of her was half full, so she got behind her in line thinking it would take a matter of minutes for her to check out. She realized her serious misjudgment. The super prepared customer in front of her handed the cashier a bulky stack of coupons. It was too late to back up. As usual, always in a rush, she had already emptied her entire cart. Which had been filled to the brim, as her initial goal to buy diapers had turned into an overflowing cart. She had grabbed everything that had caught her eyes along the way to the diaper section and from there to the exit. With a couple swift detours by the dairy and household product aisles. The winter temperatures converted her van's trunk into a suitable fridge during that season and she was very proud of how much she had managed to throw in her cart in a matter of minutes.

"We will be good for a few days," she thought.

Her sense of accomplishment got altered when she gaped at the cashier that had to scan and check a minimum a hundred coupons one by one. For some, he even had to call his manager who was nowhere to be found. The whole thing took about twenty minutes. Her child started crying. She had time to analyze her inability to have the right coupons at the right time. She was so impressed with such organization that it kept her busy and contained her anger for a while.

"She is our extreme coupon lady!" mentioned the cashier once the lady had left.

She was not sure how much the woman had saved but she saw her leaving after handing the cashier just a few dollars. Back in her car, she kept a bitter feeling for a while, she thought about a coupon for yoghurts that she had cut out and left at home. She realized how after a few years year she still did not quite master the art of juggling in the American consumer society. She was upset to think she was always the only stupid person to pay everything full price. The next day, to console herself, she swung by Dunkin Donuts just to be able to tell herself that she had used a coupon after all.

Grounded

For several years, they lived with the feeling that they were passing through, in a sort of extended transit before the next move to another destination or back to where they belonged. They were there for just one or a few more years, driven by the desire to do and discover as much as possible before the potential repatriation, before it was too late. Everything was so new, that she resumed her old habit to write down what they were going through as a family, not knowing where that would take her or what she would do with those notes, certain that those moments had to be captured somehow. They didn't quite look like tourists, but they didn't blend in with locals either. They were floating in a bizarre uncertainty which prevented any deep attachment. They enjoyed the company of others like them, also gliding in the same timeless parenthesis. Certain holidays were milestones that would bring them back to the reality of time passing and the ineluctable expiration of the

61

stay.

Years kept passing. Some families would come and go, but all the while they became more and more anchored. They engaged into robust friendships that were not meant to fade away. At some point, for the children, more years had been spent in this country than where they had come from. Parents would surprise themselves by dreaming in English, praying in English, counting in English, occasionally at first, then consistently. New Jersey was no longer a destination, it was a state of mind, inherent to who they were, to who they had become.

They always enjoyed returning to France for short stays. But the year was no longer centered on that founding trip, as they no longer believed they belonged elsewhere, nor to one place. The word "forever" was not in their vocabulary. They had settled down, but the door to new horizons would always remain open, including in their children's minds that had been nourished with an appreciation for cultural differences and open-mindedness.

Infancy

The Parisian Life - 2000 and Hereafter

"Only the children know what they are looking for"

Antoine de Saint-Exupéry – Le Petit Prince

Race of a Lifetime

"You just need to have a door you can slam! In your studio-apartment, is there at least one door you can slam?" inquired her friend who had made it to the altar.

"Really?"

"Yeah, you know. You get mad, you slam a door and everything gets better. That's how it works."

"List all the faults you see in him. Then imagine that none of these will go away. On the contrary, time will amplify them. If you are fine with that, then, that means you are ready to take the leap."

Strengthened by all the random recommendations and the enchantment of multiple marriages in their age group, they felt their own wings spreading. His grandmother had granted her blessing after the first time he brought his fiancé for dinner, admiring that she had eaten a whole fish sorting, without flinching, through the skin and bones. The rite of passage in his Italian family had been overcome. They were now ready to commit to the race of a lifetime even though they were only warming up and heading to the starting line. They chose the south of France, the Provence region, far from the Parisian grey melancholy. It was his land; she had been seduced by its warm tones, the cicadas' melodies and the lavender fragrances. Vague memories remained, such as the to-do list, annotated and highlighted over and over. There was the venue booking, the invitations, menu, flowers, clothing, rings, shoes and music choices, church meetings, town hall paperwork, just to name a few. And needless to say, arguments, lots of arguments, about the invitations, menu, flowers, clothing, ring, shoes and music decisions. Family quarrels followed one another, about who to invite or not, who could be seated with whom. But in the end and after all these hurdles, the day came and went by in a blink. The images would roll around in their heads like a series of flashes. They remembered saying yes, they recalled their sweaty hands holding each other, petals spread on the steps of the church. Some people were last minute no-shows; some weren't invited in the first place. Hugs, kisses, laughter, casual conversations, dancing, a spinning room, starving once everything was over. Years after, time polished the edges, yet one memory was still vivid. The different tables had been named after the countries participating in the latest soccer world cup. By a combination of fortuitous circumstances, a group of Italian aunts found themselves seated at the *Chile* table. *Chile* was spelled in French, *Chili*, which in Italian reads 'kili' and sounds like 'kilos'. The Italian aunts complained for years after about the affront of being associated with the notion of weight.

The Right Time

After work, she and her best girlfriend often extended the day with pre-dinner drinks at a tiny bar that was just outside the Place Clichy metro station. They would often order a glass of wine and fries with extra salt. Despite being best friends, they had many points of disagreement, mainly in the political and religious fields. But there was one matter on which they agreed hands down: fries and salad had to be generously salted. So many circumstances had brought their destinies together: same field of education, same big corporation for their first internship, same apprehension with their mothers having health issues, both married a year apart. And there they were, on that day, recapping on the highs and lows at work, as well as discussing the first months of being wives.

"Has the whole pregnancy thing ever crossed your mind yet?"

"Yes, it has. It gives me anxiety though. I feel I'm already struggling to get through my day on my own, how could I add another human being into my life? I feel I have to wait for the timing to be right. But if we think about it that way, it is never going to be the right time, you know?"

"The same thoughts are going around in circles in my head."

"And the clock is running."

"I know… Should we just take the plunge?"

"I mean, is the timing ever going to be better than now?"

"Probably not."

And so, that night, over a glass of wine and well-salted fries, the two friends decided to start the most transformative chapter of their lives, the chapter of motherhood. Years later, they would reflect on life before their children were part of it and would realize they could not even picture it anymore. It was as if their kids had always been fundamental components, even before conception.

New Life

She got confirmation that she was expecting on a bright autumn evening. Before the test came back positive, she knew. In the heart of Paris, at the Auber train station, she was going down the escalator when all of a sudden, she felt an incommensurable love. A tiny human being, not even measurable, not even identified, had started her journey. She had the undeniable certainty from the start. The positive test, then the sonogram at the doctor's made the fact sink-in. Like everybody else, they heard and read about the miracle of a new life. But the whole notion felt quite unreal until it took them to the guts. They went out that night to celebrate. Many months before, he had made reservations for 'Les folies Bergères', this touristic Parisian show, that they thought they had to see at least once in their lives.

"When I booked these tickets three months ago, I was far from imagining what we would be celebrating!" He said, still in disbelief and shaken but transported by some sort of euphoria.

"I know!" Her voice was light and confident. For her, it had always been in the cards. At that moment, she pushed her glass of wine towards him.

That night gave way to weeks of nausea, vomiting, insomnia and discomfort. The idea that this little piece of life was growing made the experience bearable. A few weeks passed by and she got used to it. She learned to tame the nausea, anticipate blood pressure drops and enjoy her never ending clothing needs in line with the little growing bump. No matter what, this new human would never stop being the most important, unforgettable part of her life.

Advent, First

The sun had not risen and she woke up all of a sudden with this odd sensation that she needed to go to the bathroom. She then came back to the bed thinking how peculiar it was that she wasn't feeling anything anymore. A few minutes passed by and this strange sensation grew in her again. That's when she understood that her baby was signaling her imminent arrival. She turned the light on, waking him up from his deep sleep.

"Hey, I think I just had two contractions in a row, let's count."

"Wait, what? Oh, ok."

He started the timer and not even five minutes later that painful wave inside her climbed again.

"This is not even five minutes; we need to run to the hospital now."

The nine months lengthy wait was coming to an end. It was surreal and thrilling. Contrary feelings seized them, both euphoria and panic. In less than the time it took for the next surge to appear, they were out of the house, hailing a taxi. Thank God, she had her bag of necessities ready at the door, just as the book she had been reading religiously for the past nine months recommended. The pain was blurring her thoughts now. There was a man ahead of them at the taxi station. It took a glance for him to understand that he had to let them go first.

"Breathe, we're almost there." Usually so sure of himself, at that moment he felt helpless.

"If she's about to have the baby, I'm not taking her!" said the taxi driver in a rather unpleasant tone.

"What? No, she's having contractions, but don't worry, she won't have the baby in your cab." And the other man now waiting for the next taxi: "Come on, man, as much as I'd rather you take me, you cannot refuse them!"

"Ok," said the taxi driver, "but if there is any damage in my cab you will be responsible for it," he roared.

The hospital was a few minutes' drive; it took two contractions in the back seat for them to make it. For her, time was now measured in contraction units as the world around got blurrier.

Advent, Then

The midwife welcomed them with a calm wide smile although she couldn't hide that a lot was going on. The sky was still dark. Soon enough she was placed in a room, summoned to breathe, while all she could think of was how nauseous she was feeling. He was standing by her side feeling a deep helplessness invade him. An hour later, she was plugged into all sorts of sensors monitoring every single vital sign, both hers and the baby's. At least now there were screens for him to watch. His scientific mind was captivated by all the waves.

"Hey, there is a contraction coming," he said, all excited. She stared at him and that was enough to make him understand how careful he needed to be.

"I know, you idiot!" The words coming out of her mouth sounded hostile, but he knew they reflected the pain that gripped her from within. Her aunt had warned her, you might curse at everyone, but that's ok, that's the one time in your life you are allowed to. The idea of giving birth without anesthesia had crossed her mind but was now forgotten.

"Where is the anesthesiologist?"

"They went to look for him." The feeling of being useless was growing stronger in him by the minute.

"Why is it taking so long? Make yourself useful, go see what's going on."

The anesthesiologist arrived and asked him to leave the room during the procedure, which seemed more reasonable anyway considering how he had almost passed out the day they were given the technical details. The mere idea of this needle into her spine was unbearable for his very visual imagination. When he came back into the room, the serenity was astonishing, a breathtaking contrast with the scene he had left. She was calm and peaceful. A few hours passed, then came the time to push, a baby's cry, tears, laughter, a baby girl on her chest.

"Am I going to know what to do?"

"Yes, you know what to do, better than anybody else. Just follow your instinct and if you have doubts, choose one person, only one, that's the most important. It can be your mother, your friend, your neighbor and that's the person you listen to, not anyone else."

Those were the words from her friend at work, which proved to be the best advice of all.

Advent, Lastly

"Should I carry her when she cries, or should I let her self-soothe?" She questioned in the presence of a few relatives visiting from abroad after she had returned home.

"When your baby cries, just take her into your arms, hug her, kiss her all you can. And don't question yourself on and on. Time flies and, soon enough, she will be a teenager and won't want anything to do with you. So, you might as well take advantage of it now that you can."

When her uncle said these words, she didn't initially realize how much they would resonate throughout her life.

Free as a Bird

It was the first time she was stepping out of the house since getting back from the hospital. Way before the birth, her house had been filled of people with good intentions: her parents, her in-laws, day visitors of all kinds. The Mexican tradition recommended forty days bedridden after labor. There was no way she would adhere to such a rule. But after two days of being sleep deprived in a full house, she was on the verge of blowing up.

"Give me the baby!" her mother-in-law had summoned the night before. These words would arouse anger in the young mother. What she needed was for someone to volunteer to go buy toilet paper.

"How is it possible for toilet paper rolls to vanish so quickly?!" she responded, which left her mother-in-law puzzled. But nobody seemed concerned.

So, that morning, she took a shower, entrusted her sleeping

baby to her mother-in-law and rushed outside. When she took her first steps out onto the street, the fresh breeze felt exhilarating. For a few seconds, she felt as if she were coming out of an elevator after being trapped in it for an entire night. Although that had never happened to her, she figured the feeling would be comparable. All the sensations she started perceiving seemed in harmony and even the unpleasant ones turned enjoyable. The street agitation mixing morning chilliness, sewer emanations, freshly baked bread were intermingled in a thrilling and invigorating way. The discordant sounds were also blending in this symphony of emotions. The frantic steps of a woman rushing to catch her bus, a delivery man at the end of the street, construction work on the other side. Life running its course. The typical Parisian sky loaded with clouds, punctured at times by a luscious ray of sunshine. She felt free and accomplished like never before. And for the first time in her entire life, she was grateful to have to go buy toilet paper.

Spell

This was the first time she was venturing out with her new-born baby girl. For the occasion, she had bundled her up in soft washed blankets. Neat and warm in her stroller, her baby girl was comfortable and peacefully sleeping. As she was waiting in line at the post office, a homeless man leaned over the stroller. His face radiated wisdom and kindness, but his attire was filthy. Her mother's instinct was deterred by the man. At that moment, the man, leaning in even closer, whispered:

"I would give anything to be in her shoes."

Seized with both deep empathy and profound disgust, she looked at him with a nervous smile and ran out of the building, postponing the postage to sometime in the future. The poor man's indigence pained her, but it also represented a scary aspect of the world in which her child would grow up and from which she wanted to shield her. Later that day, as she was falling asleep, she recalled the scene and could not help but shiver picturing the individual. It wasn't so much the fact that he was homeless that bothered her. It was as if he embodied an elf or a male fairy leaning over the cradle ready to cast a spell, from which she had been able to flee just in time. In her hypersensitive new mother brain even the most innocent encounters were taking fantastical qualities.

Next-door

The end of her maternity leave was approaching. She was still immersed in a safe bubble and was meandering across the internet when someone banged on her front door. The awakening from her day-reveries was chilling. Why didn't this person use the doorbell? The soft chime was so much more amiable than this violent fist drumming her armored door. The baby didn't wake up.

"Who is it?" she said through the door.

"It's me, Michel, your neighbor." Answered a voice that sounded familiar. "I locked myself out of my apartment."

Now reassured, she opened the door and found herself face to face with the young man, exhibiting, as always, haggard circled eyes, tousled greasy hair, mismatched and wrinkled clothes. She always thought he seemed harmless though, but still peculiar, hard to read, like he was lost in a parallel world of his own.

"What can I do for you?" she questioned.

"I just need to make a phone call; do you mind if I use your phone?"

"Of course, please. Follow me, it's right here." She stated, while directing him to the kitchen and pointing to the antique-looking device on the wall.

"Thank you very much, I appreciate it."

With that, she left the kitchen, half-closing the door to give him some space. She sat down at her computer, while keeping an eye on the individual whom she still didn't trust. While she started roaming into her online travel exploration again, she managed to overhear minced words and unclear one-way sentences coming from the kitchen.

"Hi, it's Michel.... Good and you, how is it going?... I know we haven't seen each other in so long.... Me? I'm fine, you know, same thing, work and all.... Yeah, let's plan something soon... Ok, I'll call you back soon!... Bye."

The casual chat was light years from what she would have expected. No allusion to the fact that he was locked out, that he needed spare keys, or anything of the sort. The casual exchange, as she had perceived it, just seemed like two old friends reconnecting after not having seen each other for years. Michel came out of the kitchen with a broad smile that erased his previous gloomy expression. He thanked her again and slipped out the door as furtively as he had showed up. She distinguished him cascading down the stairs and saw him through her window exiting the building with an unprecedented determination.

For the rest of the day, she was caught in a sort of perplexity in the face of humanity's oddity. As a vulnerable mother, now in charge of another human being, the insanity of the outside world terrified her. Was she going to be able to shield her daughter from mankind's incongruity?

Modern Revolution

Taking the Parisian metro with a stroller and a baby is an experience that requires good physical condition, strategy and social skills. And, of course, not too much olfactory sensitivity—but that's a lesser evil. It has to be lived in the flesh to be understood. Most Parisian metro stations are not equipped with elevators or even escalators. With a detailed knowledge of the metro network, it is possible to strategize certain choices. For example, opt for a certain entrance rather than a more intricate one. Or choose a particular connection, knowing it entails fewer hurdles than others while leading to the same destination. Even so, the obstacle course often involves stairs, which implies folding and carrying the stroller on one arm, the baby on the other and everything that was hanging on the stroller somehow as well. Sometimes, it's just two or three tiny aimless little steps that turn out to be an infuriating and insurmountable bump. Social skills can come in handy to identify a good soul who will take pity on a struggling mother and offer to carry bits and pieces of all the equipment (most of which has no real use except to make the mother feel prepared for the most unlikely situations). Though it is important to exercise good judgment, it is just as important to put aside paranoia so as to not think that the helpful but unknown human being will run away with the diaper bag or worse. From time to time, the hardship is to be faced alone, surrounded by anonymous and indifferent crowds.

One day, after she had just hurt her back riding down some stupid stairs with her baby, the stroller and all her useless possessions, she sat on the nearest bench and started to cry. She was overcome with heat flashes and a deep disgust for the public transportation system, which had started to look like human catacombs in the bowels of the earth. The sound of the subways passing in the adjacent corridors intertwined with never-ending footsteps, laughter, snatches of conversations, throat clearing noises. Through her eyes blurred by tears, she spotted a stranger who seemed focused on a conversation… with himself. He was strolling alone and speaking. She didn't think much of it as nothing surprised her anymore when it came to the urban wildlife. It was then that she realized he was carrying a cell phone which was not commonplace at that time in Paris. Something clicked inside her: a new goal gave her the strength to get up and go home. Without delay, she would acquire a cell phone which would, with no doubt, resolve all her problems. For starters, she could call for help, or in any circumstances. She would be protected, armed behind the new cutting-edge shield.

Getting a cell phone turned out to be life changing. There were some similarities to the revolution of having a baby, in the sense that life before it became unimaginable. And yet they had survived many years without it. Much later the device would become a vital tool to monitor their teenagers' whereabouts. And they would often wonder how their own parents had overcome that stage in the pre-cellphone era.

A Slap in the Face

She was one week away from going back to work. A sensation of deep anxiety grew in her chest more and more each day. This interlude of perfect bliss with her daughter had fulfilled her. She was heading over to the pediatrician. A routine visit that would turn into her own personal psychoanalysis. She had barely stepped foot in the doctor's office when she felt the tears in her eyes. Looking at the other mothers in the waiting room, she convinced herself that she was the only one inconsiderate enough to plan on leaving her child in other hands. The doctor greeted her with her usual calm smile.

"Hi cutie," at that point she was so emotional that the simple fact that the doctor was addressing her daughter brought the tears to the next level.

"Anything in particular since the last time?"

"Well…"

At that point, it was more and more difficult for words to

come out of her mouth.

"I'm going back to work next week."

"I see, do you have everything arranged in terms of childcare?"

"Yes, but…"

"But, what?"

"I feel so sad and … guilty."

"Why?"

"Well, leaving my baby with somebody I don't know. It rips my heart."

"Do you like your job?"

"Yes, I guess."

"Ok, listen to me, there are studies that prove that children in households where both parents work are smarter, more independent and more self-driven. So, stop dwelling on the negatives, go pamper yourself with some nail polish, do your hair, a facemask, put makeup on and move along! You should even go have a drink with your friends—no husband, no baby—once in a while. Doctor's advice!" she said handing her a piece of paper where she had written the same decree as if it were a prescription. "Besides, if you stay home, you are going to spend your day picking up crumbs on the floor. Believe me, I've been there." Her face, although authoritative in appearance, reflected a certain sympathy.

The rest of the visit flew by. A little shaken by these few words that hit her mental target, she crossed the waiting room towards the exit, looking at the other moms and wondering if their kids would be less smart than hers. Deep down she was convinced that if a disconsolate stay at home mother had come in, the doctor would have delivered the opposite message about all the unconditional love that their child would get.

Regardless, she got what she needed to hear. She would still cry the night before. Then she was all of a sudden overcome with a certain excitement similar to the night before going back to school after a summer break. The day of, the nanny showed up right on time with a big, nurturing smile. She gave more than the necessary recommendations. The precise feeding times and steps to prepare the formula, the absolute need to ensure a loud and distinct burp was heard after each bottle, the cream to use in case of irritation, the ban on letting baby cry or sleep with a dirty diaper, the selection of CDs that were to be played, the small shoes to put on when going out for aesthetic purposes only. Then she dove into the fresh morning air which, without realizing it, once again invaded her with an immense feeling of freedom.

Abyss

It was a sunny Tuesday in late summer. She had just had lunch with a quite talkative colleague. The conversation had revolved around back-to-school developments, interspersed with a few stories of family vacations. An extensive long French lunch break punctuated by an espresso shot that would keep her awake for the rest of the day. She walked without conviction towards her boss' office. She and her teammate were scheduled to discuss training sessions for their counterparts in New Jersey. She was expected to travel there late October. The phone rang one first time. An IT guy informed their boss that a plane had just crashed on the twin towers in NYC. He shared the information with them, they looked at each other, a little shocked, envisioning nothing more than a terrible accident. They continued their conversation, scrolling through the calendars and everyone's availability. The phone rang a second time. The same IT guy reported that a second plane had crashed on the other twin tower, with hundreds of passengers. All of a sudden, what had seemed like an accident became a calculated terrorist attack. After a very short conversation, he hung up the phone. A few minutes of silence followed. They stared at each other, lacking words, immersed in a deluge of thoughts. In no time accessing information on the internet became impossible, everyone was on the web looking for explanations and images. In Paris rumors of similar attacks on European capitals began to circulate. Everyone was agitated, going from one office to another, seeking to put the pieces together, to make sense out of the events that were unfolding darker and darker by the minute. After an hour or so, employees received a message authorizing them to leave the office. Without even thinking, she went straight home. That day she hugged her daughter and husband much tighter than ever before.

Let It Be

The two girlfriends and colleagues had been back to work for over a year after long simultaneous maternity leaves, which acted as a kind of parenthesis in their lives, sheltering them from the world. They had also immersed themselves back into harsh realities. After months spent in a bubble of baby smells and nursery rhymes, sometimes it felt as if life was just spitting in their face. They knew they would have to stick together to tackle whatever the loathsome universe was going to throw at them. They were determined to resume their habit of sitting together for a drink after work once in a while. On this late summer evening, after making the necessary arrangements, they sat down at their usual café Place Clichy and each ordered a glass of chilled Beaujolais Village accompanied by a platter of fries to share and requested the salt container. The combination was both stimulating and soothing. Even so, the conversation started with a morose tone that evening. Both had always dreamed of multiple little ducklings. But the atrocity of the 9/11terrorist attacks had led them to question the meaning of life and whether it was right to bring more human beings to Earth. As the evening progressed, the clouds in their thoughts started to disperse and eventually cleared up. Such was the enchantment of friendship, or maybe the alchemy operated by the wine. Perhaps, it was just the influence of the warm late summer breeze. Be that as it may, after that evening, the future took a turn for the better.

New Addition

She didn't let circumstances put an end to her lifelong dream of having a big family. Soon after, a second addition came along. After a tiring pregnancy, haunted by nausea and lack of sleep, another little angel opened her eyes to the world. She had been told that second children were the fastest. It turned out to be truer than expected. She barely got the epidural, as she had demanded it in a way that only a woman about to give birth can command things. For their second, they had decided to keep the gender a surprise until birth. Everything happened so fast, that only ten minutes after the birth, as the warm little body was snuggled into her arms, filling her with indescribable euphoria, she turned to her husband and inquired:

"Is it a boy or a girl?"

With an incredulous look he revealed the evidence of what he had already known for what seemed like an eternity:

"It's a girl!"

In the midst of the overwhelming bliss, knowing the sex of her child had become of little importance compared to hearing the first breath and cry.

Back home, one of the most difficult transitions of her life was about to unfold. Organizing synchronized naps became an obsession. Like any young mother, she had learned to sleep on command as soon as her babies fell asleep, which could happen at any time of the day or night. Her life was no longer settled on a circadian rhythm but on a feed, change, nap, repeat. Having not one but two little babies, these moments seemed to her as rare as a lunar eclipse. One day, after a sleepless night and a very early awakening, when her husband was already long gone at work, she had succeeded in making the two little ones fall asleep at the same time. She had just laid down under a blanket, filled with indescribable joy, savoring this much-needed nap, when the doorbell rang. The profound inner peace turned into an uncontrollable anger. She hoped and prayed that nobody would wake up and that this impertinent intruder would give up. But the doorbell picked up a second time, then a third time more insistent and accompanied by a call:

"Hello, is somebody here?"

This was *the straw that broke the camel's back*, as they say. She got up, walked as gently as she could to the door and opened it. It was the concierge who had a package that didn't fit under the door. She was aware of all the local residents' schedules, hence her insistence at the doorbell as she was certain the young mother was inside.

"My little ones are sleeping; in the future, can you please not ring and just leave the packages in front of the door please?" she whispered with the calmest voice possible as she tried to tame her interior, which was ready to explode.

"Sorry, I thought you'd rather I did not do that," she replied with the most raucous smoker voice that could ever exist.

The damage was done. A little cry emanated from the inside. She closed the door on the woman, as well as on her hopes for that peaceful sleep. She grabbed the phone, called her husband and wept:

"If you don't come home right now, I will either commit a murder or throw something out the window."

To her greatest surprise, in record time, he opened the door with a worried face. She was watching TV and the two little ones were sleeping, one on her baby bouncer, the other cuddled on the sofa.

"What are you doing here?"

"Well, you said you were going to commit a murder."

"Oh yeah… No, I would never do that."

"Well, with your tone, I got scared."

He settled on the couch and soon they were all asleep. A calm afternoon was what this sleep deprived family needed.

Metro Jungle

She was heading to work, walking along the line 1 platform at the Gare de Lyon station. Further down she noticed a drunk woman, leaning forward with swinging arms. She was about to pass her when the woman bolted straight up and hit her left arm, nearly making her fall onto the train track. Since early childhood, she had been a deep-rooted Parisian. When it came to the crazy people that populate the metro stations and streets, she had pretty much seen it all. At the age of ten, her father had thrown her in the metro with a mission: to reach the *Institut Pasteur*. The endeavor involved switching lines and took a lot of determination, but she made it. That had marked her induction to being a Parisian to the core. Years later, the metro was still full of chaos, danger and crazy individuals. Now that she was a mother, it was as if her awareness had been sharpened. The crowded state of the wagons would always lead to vicious men groping young women.

One time, in the middle of a tight and hysterical crowd, she heard the voice of a woman exasperated by the inappropriate grope of an indelicate man rise from the opposite side of the car: "If I keep feeling it touching me, I'll cut it off!"

Some laughed, some started sweating more and all knew what was going on. Another time, the wagon door opened on a woman preaching about Jesus' coming. More times than she could count, she had changed seats, feeling uncomfortable because of a stare, someone sitting way too close, what her neighbor was reading, eating, doing; like this nervous man fingering his lips while staring at her. All these moments were engraved in her Parisian brain. She lived in a constant awareness of her surroundings while wholly diving in a book or in her notes, these notes that she grew into the habit of scribbling to make sure she would encapsule crucial moments, although most were seemingly insignificant.

One of her college friends was even more Parisian than her. Taking public transportations with him would alleviate all her fears as he would dare the most outrageous moves. One day, as she was getting on the bus, ready to sit on the first seat available, right behind the driver, her friend looked at her in disagreement and stated, "You never sit in these first seats my dear, because next thing you know, you have to leave your seat for an older person and go straight to the back."

But she was naïve and, most of all, a rule follower. One morning, giving away her seat for a woman with a prominent belly, she experienced the most shameful feeling when the woman retorted, "I'm not pregnant, I'm fat."

"It's ok, you can still sit down," she mumbled.

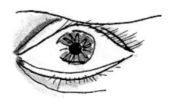

Urban Anthill

New York, Paris, Mexico … Though they may seem different, they are all filled with streets and public transport populated by suffocating crowds and bizarre individuals. Inhabitants of these megalopolis live by the same unfailing rule: never meet a stranger's eyes. One day, while walking down the Champs Elysée heading to a meeting with a provider, she broke the rule. As she was waiting at a pedestrian crossing, she turned to the woman standing next to her. Their eyes met. A glance she would never forget. While staring at her, the stranger uttered with a firm and determined voice, "We'll meet again."

The light turned green and in seconds the woman disappeared into the Parisian crowd. In this moment of vulnerability facing human neurosis, she was seized with panic and existential questions. Later at night, before turning off the light, she took a few notes on the small pad laying on her nightstand. *As if I had been struck by the look of that woman, I felt an intense need to hug my child.*

Growing Clan

They were convinced that exhaustion and sleepless nights would last forever. In a blink of an eye, their routine fell back into something simpler and the desire for a third child came. Pregnancy this time was a breeze; discomforts seemed benign and she wanted to enjoy every single moment as this could be the last one. They knew it was a girl. During the second sonogram, the doctor had asked with a big smile if they were still holding on to the skirts. Second birth had been so quick that she almost couldn't get the epidural. But this one took her time. The midwife told her that her uterus was perhaps a little tired.

"Isn't it supposed to work as much as necessary?" she responded.

She knew mothers who birthed ten or more children, so why would her system fail after two? It made no sense. Despite this unpleasant remark, the third tiny cherub saw the light of day without too much effort. Everything unfolded naturally, like the inflow of her breastmilk for which she had to wait for days the two first times. Even some of the pain went almost unnoticed, as she knew with certainty this time that it was all a succession of ephemeral moments she needed to appreciate. "*Todo pasa*" her grandmother would tirelessly repeat in Spanish. When the first and even the second child were born, these words yielded very little control over reality. But as she got older, they started to resonate more clearly in her existence. The evanescence of each moment in life became more palpable and made difficult ones easier to endure, almost pleasant.

They returned home in an atmosphere of joy. The two older ones had prepared welcome signs. And just like that, fragmented sleep was now rooted in their lives again. One morning, as she was changing a diaper, her eyes landed on two red spots that seemed like blood. She sank into panic and checked the diaper bag. In a few minutes the baby was strapped into the car seat and she was driving to the pediatrician in order to be first in line for the walk-ins. She stepped into the waiting room, where another young woman was waiting with her newborn baby.

"Is she your first?"

"Yes," she responded with a sweet and quiet voice that conveyed an unusual self-confidence, given the circumstances, "How about you?"

"She's my third."

"Does everything become easier?" she inquired with a serene tone that contrasted with her concerned look.

"I'm not sure I would say easier, but busier, yes," she responded as she watched the new mom clean her baby's eyes with an obvious sudden anxiety. "She has conjunctivitis …

Poor thing. Be careful; last time mine had it, I caught it too."

The new mother looked up, both amazed and relieved at the revelation. How had she not thought about it?! She had read about it in her multiple books, but in the midst of her worry hadn't even thought about it.

"I'm so relieved, you're right, it's just a pink eye. And you, what brings you here?"

"There were tiny blood spots in her diaper this morning."

"That's the newborn period, I read about it."

"What? What is that?"

"They say sometimes, baby girls have a tiny period due to the influx of hormones from their mother. It's a very brief thing and then she won't have it until puberty."

"She's my third daughter and I had never heard of this! See, each child comes with their own set of novelties!"

"I am glad we reassured each other!"

She realized then that though everything felt easy and smooth sailing, even experience cannot shield you from new challenges. Yet, in times of crisis, camaraderie and complicity between mothers, even not knowing each other, was often a source of reinsurance, wisdom and inner peace.

Mama Duck

Wherever she went into her neighborhood, she was like a mama duck followed by her ducklings, though the configuration was a little different. It was not a single file line with the mother in front and the little ones waddling behind, but rather a wave occupying the sidewalk in its entirety, with a baby in the stroller and two little girls holding on from either side. Although, there was often a war over who was going to walk on which side. To be honest, it did matter. She had once mentioned that the side closest to the road was more dangerous. This established in the little one's minds the idea that there was a certain privilege associated with being on the side by the wall. At the same time, being on the street side meant being recognized as more grown up and responsible. The side by the wall did come with its own set of obstacles, like the mailbox pressed up against the wall at the end of their street (on which one of them once banged her head which caused a black eye that wouldn't go away for a few weeks).

Sometimes, a little voice would complain.

"I don't want to walk anymore!"

The whole thing was followed by an outburst over how unfair it was that the baby was entitled to the stroller. But, of course, she had a few tricks up her sleeve, like swinging by the bakery. With a piece of baguette to bite on, everything would return to normal. Is there any mother who can boast of never having used blackmail as a tool to win over a child's refusal?

Scarce Commodity

Having a good night's sleep can be a relative concept. When she became pregnant for the first time, a colleague brought out an inconceivable principle that she knew would become true:

"From now on, you will never sleep soundly ever again."

The emergence of children meant the end of those lazy weekends sleeping in. They also brought along sudden nocturnal awakenings due to a multitude of events from fevers, stomachaches, earaches to thunderstorms or nightmares. She didn't know it yet, but the adolescence would later bring its own set of challenges, like late evenings spent waiting for updates from the ungrateful teens shamelessly partying while parents are fretting over their safety at home.

Circadian Cycle

It was an ordinary evening; three little ones needed to be put in bed against their pugnacious will. Last preparations had been completed, teeth had been brushed, toys whose shadows could be frightening in the dark had been stashed away and comforting stuffed animals had been unearthed from their hiding places. Last goodnight kisses were about to be distributed when the older one inquired, "How come in summer the days last longer and the nights are shorter and in winter the nights are longer and the days are shorter?"

The Cartesian mind of the father was triggered. He rushed to grab different size balls and started explaining the solar system. Calling his wife to the rescue, both initiated a choreography of planets rotating around the sun. He revealed the notions of orbits and gravitation. The look on their daughter's face gave away her perplexity. Although part of her was enjoying this beautiful ballet that was delaying her bedtime, she was puzzled, not fully understanding how all this was in any way linked to her initial question.

"I don't understand."

"Look, the orbit of the earth around the sun is tilted, during summer…"

Her anxiety was growing.

"I'm scared, I won't be able to sleep."

Ok, that's enough, this is not the time nor the place for an astronomy lesson, she thought and with the calmest and sweetest voice, she sat next to her daughter and said, "During summer the sun is super happy and full of energy, but the moon is very tired and sleepy. Therefore, we see the sun much more. But during winter, the sun is very tired of all the activity it had during summer, so it goes to bed early and we see it less. The moon in winter is super energized and shows itself longer."

Satisfied with that explanation, she kissed her parent's goodnight, hugged her baby doll and turned to the wall, closing her tired little eyes. Somewhat vexed, but also relieved, he thought to himself that he would come back to the case when her mind would be more receptive. And so, he did, but much later.

Once Upon a Big Bad Funny Wolf

It was bedtime as usual. The light had been turned off, when a small voice arose:

"I'm scared."

"It's time to sleep, there is no reason to be scared."

"But I'm scared."

"What are you scared of?"

"I'm scared of the wolf."

"There is no wolf in the house. And there are not even wolves in this area. Mom and Dad are right here, this is the safest place on Earth." Her tone projected a subtle blend of emotions: the empathy of an understanding mother and the annoyance of a human being who only aspires to sleep.

She gave her a good night kiss for the fourth time and left, leaving the door half open and the hallway light on. A few minutes passed. She was convinced and relieved that the potential storm that was her daughter's insistence on the wolf's presence had been tamed until a sob broke through the silence once more:

"I'm scared."

"I told you there are no wolves around here. Wolves live very far away, they don't even like it here. There are too many houses, they are scared of humans, you know…"

"But, in school we read this story about a little girl and her grandma. They get eaten by a wolf."

"Little Red Riding Hood? That's an old tale, it's not real."

"But I'm scared there is a wolf under my bed."

"Ok, let's look together."

She turned the light on and they both looked under the bed. The little girl seemed reassured; her adult eyes were struck by the layer of dust that she made a mental note to take care of later. The little one climbed back into her bed half convinced. She ended up falling asleep. Every single night, the same ritornello would unfold. She soon realized that the fear of the wolf had not just arisen from that one-time story; the teacher had a whole unit on the wolf. All the classic tales centered on wolves were studied one after the other. The word wolf ('loup' in French) was used as a key word to dissect the sound 'ou' different from 'o' or 'u' in the French language. Each day that passed, parents were trying in vain to tame the fear while the teacher kept on fueling it. She scheduled an appointment with the teacher during which she explained the issue she was facing. She asked the teacher if she could help alleviate the fear, or even downright change the subject. The teacher retorted that it was a rite of passage for the child to overcome the "fear of being devoured." With this disturbing edict, she left wondering whether she herself had ever overcome that fear.

The angst in her eldest would pass. But two years later, the little sister entered kindergarten with the same teacher. She started worrying about the idea that the whole "fear of being devoured" situation would come back. One evening, around the same time of the school year that the unit on the wolf had started two years before, as she was saying goodnight, the little one started the conversation:

"Can I tell you something?"

"Of course!"

"We read this story in school today and it was so funny."

"What was the story?"

"There was this wolf; and at the end of the story, he eats the grandma, it was hilarious!"

That evening, she grasped how unique and different human beings each of her children were.

Buzet

The adults were sitting at the dining room table talking. The children had long since finished eating. They were playing, running from one room to another, disappearing upstairs or down into the basement. Too long a silence would raise concern at times. But for the most part, the parents were careful not to investigate too much and rather enjoy the precious and fleeting adult time. They even tacitly agreed to call the kids for dessert well after they had savored it themselves. Deep inside, she hoped she would not suffer too much from the consequences of the tornado that may have ransacked the house while she enjoyed the peaceful time. It was in the middle of that train of thought that their little one climbed onto his lap and rested her head against his shoulder. Her small voice emerged:

"BU – ZET."

"What did you just say?"

The child looked at her dad, proud and repeated with

confidence:

"BUZET."

The entire table was now captivated.

"It's the wine. It's the name of the wine!"

The magnum of vintage 'Buzet' red wine sitting on the table was now the center of attention. It had never occurred to him that his five-year-old daughter could already read. She was then put to the test of deciphering numerous words written on the objects at hand, which she performed without making even the slightest mistake. And so, they realized that behind her shy demeanor, she had learned to read on her own long before her peers. No doubt the motivation for that had been triggered by the idea of doing as well as her bigger sister. Shortly after, the call for reading became an insatiable hunger for books that she would consume for years on end. Years later, as a teenager, growing up in the suburbs of New York, she would beg her parents to let her take the train to the city to go dream for hours in the mother of all bookstores in her eyes: The Strand. Sometimes, she would settle for a tiny local bookstore. Surrounded by books, she would always feel at home.

Chickenpox

They were almost done packing for their one-month trip to Asia. Every detail had been thought through. Each item in the extensive checklist had been crossed out. She grabbed the little stuffed cow and bunny, both still laying down on the sofa and threw them on top of the carry-on bag. The carry on was dedicated to important items such as passports, phones, money and of course, her daughters' vital comforting personas. The two youngest would go nowhere without the Little Cow and Bunny. They were both old, filthy and squished. Bunny's right arm had even been amputated due to being chewed to the point of destruction but was nonetheless still deeply cherished.

"Little Cow is not coming with us to China."

She turned around and noticed her daughter was taking Little Cow out of the bag with a sharp determination.

"What do you mean she is not coming?"

"She can't, she has chickenpox."

She laid Little Cow on the couch pillow and went back to play as if nothing abnormal had happened. As cute as that may have seemed, a few minutes later, the cautious mother grabbed Little Cow and put it back in the bag, not without making sure that the gesture had gone unnoticed. An hour later, from the kitchen, she heard: "Why did you put Little Cow back in your bag? I told you she is sick and she can't travel," she rambled while picking up her stuffed animal and bringing it back to the couch.

"Are you sure you don't want her to come with us? Once we leave, we are going to be very far away and we will not be able to come back to get her. So, you will not have her to sleep with you, nor in the plane, nor anywhere."

"Yes, I'm sure. She has chickenpox and she is contagious, so she will be much better off here."

And so, during the whole month-long expedition, Little Cow remained safe and sound at home. Not once was she mentioned, not once did the parents feel that she was missed. A long separation, which would have seemed unimaginable happened without regrets. A month passed by and then came the day of their return. As the plane landed its wheels on the runway, she opened her sleepy little eyes. In no time, a bright and spirited emotion emanated from them:

"I can't wait to see my Little Cow again!" She whispered with obvious excitement.

The reunion was poignant after an entire month of hibernating emotions. Weeks had passed by. Time, distance and travel had made the child grow up. The affection for the Little Cow would always be special. The process for it to evolve into a childhood keepsake had started to run its course. Bunny, who had had the privilege of taking part in the journey, remained

an essential family member for a few more years, before join-
ing Little Cow in the memory box.

Big Bang

The family of five roamed around the world as usual. They were sitting on a bus that was taking them back from the Great Wall to the center of Beijing. Two of the little ones had entered that age where every day is punctuated by an incessant ballet of questions. Being in a foreign country would only arouse their natural curiosity more. "Why do people smoke so much? Why is there fog? What happens if...? Could we get lost? Will I die if I drink this? Can a mosquito give me a disease? Can ticks attack humans?" Depending on the circumstances and the level of patience at that very moment, every question was likely to open infinite discussions through which the children would deepen their awareness of their environment, along with its mysteries and dangers. But that particular day turned out to be different from all others. As landscapes were passing before their astonished eyes, those of a city undergoing massive upheaval to host the Olympic Games a few months later, a tiny voice rose:

"How was the universe created?"

"There was a big explosion, called the Big Bang, in which all the galaxies with their stars and planets were created" responded her dad with conviction.

"Yes. I know that. But what happened *before* that?"

Green Soup Makes Children Grow Up

"*A table*," she yelled.

The little ones ran downstairs to the rallying maternal signal that diner was ready.

"What's for dinner?" They inquired in unison.

"Delicious vegetable soup," she responded.

"Why is it green? I like it when it's orange."

"I don't like green soup."

"I don't want soup."

Their initial joint enthusiasm at the idea of having dinner subsided as quickly as it had manifested itself. They liked it so much better when there were fries or pasta rather than green soup. The moods became grumpy. The meal turned into a battle.

She raised her voice, threatened, then tried bribery. "If you eat half your bowl, I will let you watch TV before bed."

She conceded in despair. The oldest ended up ingesting the greenish concoction. The youngest deployed a complicated strategy that involved dipping in small balls of bread and drinking lots of water in between spoonfuls. The struggle had paid off. However, the middle one's face indicated an irreducible refusal hidden behind a deep silence.

"I want you to try it. One spoonful, that's it. And if you don't like it, that's fine, we will move on."

The other two found the idea that their sister would get away with just tasting the soup particularly unfair, but they didn't flinch. It was because you never knew. They were at a critical turning point. They had won the battle of only having to eat half a bowl. Some kind of backtracking in their mother's verdict was not unheard of and could result in having to swallow the other half, so it was better to stay quiet.

It was at that very moment of uncertainty that a clumsy nudge pushed the untouched soup bowl to the ground. The floor was now covered in small pieces of porcelain and green liquid mix.

Enough was enough. The angry mother took her by the hand and locked her in the bathroom.

"You are in time out until further notice," she stipulated, "Think about your attitude."

In the end, the little one won her case. She knew her mother wouldn't let her go to bed with an empty stomach. After a while, she was offered yogurt and an apple, but only after she had apologized for the broken bowl. It was more than enough to get through the night. Yet there was a lot of left-over green pottage since no one had wanted it. So, the next day, she warmed up the potion again.

"*A table*," she called, as usual.

In a flash, the three hungry little faces showed up in the kitchen. As soon as her eyes made contact with the cooking pot, the strong headed mind turned around and locked herself in the bathroom, indicating with that action even more determination than the day before, a resounding and uncompromising no.

A few years later, she would end up eating and even loving her mother's green soup. *You need to try seven times to end up liking something* was the old French adage they always believed in and had adhered to with their children. They often wondered if food rejections had anything to do with the color green. That particular color always required more persuasion and vigilance. One day, while she was cleaning behind a kitchen cabinet, she noticed with horror a sticky mass of what seemed to have been kiwis, now in the process of advanced decomposition. Deeply repulsed, she summoned the kids. Everyone denied any responsibility in the matter, but she had her suspicions about the culprit.

"I'm a little worried," she said out loud, giving the impression of talking to herself, "because with food like this behind the furniture, we will have mice wandering the house."

No further development took place until the evening, other than her eldest displaying a very taciturn demeanor. A few hours had passed when she presented herself to her mother with a contrite look and a confession. It was her, she was sorry, but first and foremost terrified at the prospect of coming face to face with a mouse. Therefore, she indicated a few other places where she had made unwanted food disappear. Green was predominant but not exclusive. Peas and kiwis were in the mix. Those ended up being accepted a few years later. Beets and cantaloupe, on the other hand, although having been tasted more than seven times, remained banished from her plate. The adage was efficient, but not infallible.

Domino Effect

"Can you please bring me my purse that's in the living room?" whispered the mom to the oldest while blocking the speaker on the telephone handset; she was on hold with the operator.

"Why?" She inquired in a cheeky tone.

"Because I'm asking you to do it and because I'm busy here and I need your help," she answered.

Interrupting her game, she turned to her younger sister.

"Can you go get mom's purse from the living room?" Her mother had resumed her telephone conversation and was unaware of what was taking place, but the oldest still murmured to ensure her mother would not hear.

"Why? Mom asked you," she retorted, annoyed.

"Because I'm asking you. Mom and I are busy and we need your help," she decreed.

Dragging her feet, she started to walk towards the living room when her little sister appeared. She decided to take a chance.

"Hey, can you go get mom's purse in the living room?" she asked with authority.

"Why?" She mumbled.

"Because if you do, you will be the queen forever," she said, persuading her like only a big sister can.

As it was often the case, all this happened away from the mother's eyes, no one was reprimanded. Such is life and power games among siblings.

Introspection

As she walked through the hallways, carrying on with her day at work, going mentally through her unachievable to-do list, she realized how unreasonable it was for her to always want to be in control of everything. Things were not always going to be done the way she would have done them. However, chances were, they were going to be alright. She should have known that by now; she had nannies when her kids were younger and at the end of the day, she would often come home to find that her kids' skirts and t-shirts did not always match—at least not in the way she wanted it. But the kids were safe and happy that they were able to pick out their own clothes for once. Above all, they were delighted to enjoy a little freedom in the otherwise autocratic world their mother had created.

She started browsing through an old notebook. *Ceux que l'on met au monde ne nous appartiennent pas. Those we bring into the world do not belong to us.* That was the title of a Linda Lemay song, this Quebecois singer she loved. It had made her shed a few tears during her pregnancy and she had made sure to mark those words down. Reading them brought back vivid memories of her as a young mother. Through those words, she could sense every bit of those instants. But it is only at this precise moment of her life that the words truly resonated in her mind. Her children were growing inch by inch every day, stealthily leaving the nest, belonging to her less and less, becoming fully-fledged human beings.

Adolescence

The New Jersey Life - 2015 and Hereafter

"All grown-ups were once children first. But few of them remember it"

Antoine de Saint-Exupéry – Le Petit Prince

The Biggest Sister

Having dropped everyone off at school; the mother swung by her house to grab her laptop that she had forgotten in the morning rush and a piece of a leftover muffin she knew was still on the counter. As she was entering the driveway, the familiar face of a prodigious woman shaking a rug on the side porch appeared. It made her happy. In her mind, she was her fairy godmother. She had the magical power, so to speak, to turn chaos into order every week. They exchanged a few words in Spanish.

"¿Como están los niños? ¿Mucho trabajo?"

She cherished those brief morning exchanges, as they were both foreigners to the American culture who loved their American way of life. They both saw it through critical lenses, having grown up in a different cultural environment. She knew she had to hurry up and cut the conversation short. As she was hopping into the car, her phone vibrated: her oldest daughter, a freshman in high school, was begging her to pick her up as soon as possible. A critical situation had arisen. She needed to come home to wash her hair that was greasy. Since she had realized it, she was hiding in the bathroom. Another one of those situations where she wished there was a parenting manual for some guidance. She mumbled in her car, "I can't pick her up just because her hair is greasy! And then I have to wait! She won't go back to school with wet hair! I have to be at work and she needs to learn that life is not so sugar coated."

"Is everything alright?" she heard as she was sitting in her car, drowning in her thoughts.

"My older one wants me to pick her up from school because she realized her hair is greasy!"

"That's unfortunate. So, you're going to go get her?"

"But I can't, it's already so late, this is insane!"

Her softhearted, somewhat pushover side took over. She was easily persuaded by the words of this other mother just as indulgent as her. She realized how miserable her daughter probably was. For a moment, she put herself in her shoes. Adolescence was such a rough passage. She picked her up and drove her home, hugged her as she stated this was a one-time thing. As ungrateful as a teenager can be, deep inside, her daughter was left with the absolute certainty that her mother would be there for her no matter what. Their fairy godmother drove the teenager to school an hour later, now with a smile on her face and squeaky-clean hair.

The Bigger Sister

"Do you think that the dishes that you just threw in the sink will migrate all alone into the dishwasher with their little legs?" Although she could have considered herself lucky that the dishes were at least in the sink and not still on the table, that day, she was particularly irritable. The previous Sunday, with her girlfriend, they had visited a bunch of open houses just for fun. She knew the houses had been staged to look impeccable. But the sight of these flawless houses, worthy of an interior design magazine, had made her acutely aware of the fact that her house was the very definition of chaos and clutter.

"Ugh, Mom, I don't have time," replied the teenager with that insolent tone which was at its peak on school mornings.

"And you think I have time?" she responded, but the young teenager had already run upstairs, ignoring her mother's lecture.

That morning, a clothing crisis was unfolding. The mother

decided to just postpone the kitchen sermon to another time as she witnessed the situation, feeling both helpless and moved, reflecting on how teenage years could be such a difficult time.

"You know we have to leave soon, right?" she ventured to say.

The young girl slammed the bathroom door. The outfit she had prepared the night before was now on the floor.

"I can't wear this." She heard her say, "where are my jean shorts?"

The mother knew damn well that those were in the dirty laundry hamper but decided not to say anything so as to not stir up the precarious mood. The young lady looked more self-conscious than the night before. Was it because of a bad dream or because of what that girl had told her the day before? At the dinner table, she had shared how hurtful it had been and how she couldn't stand her, always so vain, rude and sassy. As a mother, she knew that whenever she would be able to take a step back, she would feel more pity than anything else for that girl. She had instilled in her to be happy with who she was and not to envy those who cared about popularity and boys. Even so, every day her self-esteem was put to the test. Hearing from her mom that she was the most beautiful girl in her grade was often meaningless. On good days, her older sister would also tell her she was pretty. She trusted her a little more.

She had now moved onto putting more effort into her hair and make-up. But it was almost time to leave and she still hadn't figured out what to wear. At that point, she had emptied every single shelf of her closet and still looked unsure. Now, in her mother's heart, empathy started to be chipped with despair as she realized how her closet had thrown up everything that was inside. Her room was a battlefield. A once perfect setting was now destroyed by a tornado of adolescence uncertainties. The dream of a perfectly staged house was drifting away by the minute.

Later that day, as she was grocery shopping, she ran into a woman who's kids her daughter had babysat multiple times. She was full of praise, stating her daughter was the most amazing kid, she would always enjoy coming back home after she babysat her kids, as her kitchen was neater and cleaner than ever. To these words she felt proud thinking that somehow, despite her doubts, she had managed to do some things right. However, part of her was perplexed. How was it that she was the one always seeing the worst of her kids?

The Big Sister

It was no longer a secret for anyone that a fourth musketeer was on the way. One morning at the breakfast table, the little 7-year-old perspicacious mind inquired, "I have a question, my little brother is inside you … and he comes from you and dad, right?"

"Yes, that's right."

"But dad is not inside you…"

The silence was heavy.

"How did he get inside you then?"

At that point of parental mutism, came the biggest sister to the rescue.

"You'll learn that when you get the Talk in 5th grade."

She was referring to the famous Talk that children in the United States get at the end of elementary school. When their eldest got the Talk, they had just moved to America from France. They did wonder for a while what the content of the

Talk had been since their kid of course didn't share a word of it, besides the fact that boys and girls had been split into two different groups. The night prior to it, they had had to sign a form stating that they agreed for their child to attend. One day, she had asked another mom, "What do they tell the kids during the Talk?"

"It depends on the health teacher. When I got the Talk as a kid, she told us everything."

The other mom's answer did not dissipate all the questions she had, so they remained unresolved. But her oldest daughter putting an end to the questions of the youngest that morning blessed the parents with the greatest relief. The little one didn't pursue the inquiry further, seeming satisfied with the idea that she would get the answer somehow. Or maybe she already had an idea that needed to be confirmed but sensed that the timing was not right. Being the youngest of three sisters, she had always found the way to get what she wanted in situations where her older sisters would have faced a prohibitory wall.

"Mom, you had me wait until I was in 8th grade to be able to watch *Friends*. You were sitting next to me and fast-forwarding inappropriate scenes! Now she is in 6th grade and she is watching it alone on her iPad."

"I know... I'm not proud of it," she answered.

And it's true, she wasn't proud of it. Parents try their best to be fair, to apply the same rules and treatments, but somehow the way they raise each child is in no way comparable. Not without reason, a friend of hers from Human Resources told her that if she were to ask only one question to candidates she was interviewing to be hired, it would be whether they had siblings and where they fell within the family. She was convinced that this information alone would give way more insight on team behavior and performance than any academic or professional background.

Sister's Brawl

The girls were scheduled for portraits at the dance studio that afternoon. She had made sure there were enough tights, hair nets, bobby pins, hair ties and foundation for an entire army of dancers. Everything was running smoothly… until it wasn't. She had just managed to twist hair up into a bun that satisfied the youngest, which was kind of a miracle, when out of the blue, screaming and crying burst from everywhere.

"She stole my flat iron!"

"Why is she using my eyeshadow? It's disgusting!"

"It's *my* eyeshadow, mom bought it for *me*!"

"No, it isn't, you're a liar." Thus, starting the fireworks of name-calling.

"Last week you took my mascara and I didn't say anything!"

"That's because I take care of things I borrow. You lost my black sweater; you're not borrowing anything ever again."

"You're so selfish!"

The screaming intensified, becoming out of control within seconds. Curse words flew like confetti. The two young girls were each holding one end of the flat iron, like two vicious dogs fighting over a stick. Teeth and claws were showing. After uttering ineffective threats, the mother sat down. On her cheeks, she felt tears beginning to ooze. The father intervened to disengage the tussle.

They were late to the portrait session. The girls had somehow managed to look impeccable. The buns were flawless, not a single frizzy hair. In contrast, the apathetic mother was the female version of Charlie Chaplin, blown out by the Billows Feeding Machine. Her eyes sunk in her eyelids, circled in gray. She realized her sweatshirt was stained and ripped.

"Sorry we're so late," she muttered. "I thought they were going to kill each other."

The woman at the reception who was a mother of three daughters herself, immersed in the nostalgia of those teenage quarrels and moved by the mother in distress, responded, "I remember those days. I too thought they were going to kill each other a couple times. But I promise you one thing, soon they will be best friends."

Health Class

It was a dark winter evening. While the engine was still running and the heat was on, they were waiting for the youngest sister to come out of her friend's house. Although she had told her she would be there at six sharp and she needed to be at the door, it always took forever. Not only her, they were all the same. Their phones were implanted in their hands, but when it was their mother texting or calling, they never saw it right away. Propitiously, this gave her and the older sister waiting time to talk a little. A teenager's openness to talk can come out at the most unexpected times. *You gotta be ready for it*!

"Who did you have lunch with today?"

"I went to work study."

"Ah!"

"I hate the math teacher; she doesn't explain anything and expects us to understand on our own."

"That's annoying."

"And this boy who sits next to me, every time he talks, he sounds like he's having an orgasm…"

"What did you just say?!"

The teenager looked at her mother. She didn't look surprised or guilty but aware of the cause of disconcert.

"Yeah, you know, like moaning."

"How do you even know what that means and what it sounds like?"

"We learned that in health class."

"You learned what an orgasm is?" She was a little baffled to realize the depth that health talks would go into.

"Yeah."

"How did the teacher bring that up? What was the lesson about?"

"Well, the teacher told us to write down all our questions and she went over each one and explained everything."

"That's good, so you know everything?"

"Yes."

"I'm glad to hear that."

"And at the end it was funny, because once she answered all our questions, she asked us if there was anything else that was left unanswered. This kid raised his hand. The teacher said, 'yes, what else do you want to know?' And he said, 'well, this is all fine, but there is one thing we haven't talked about.' 'Ok, what is that?' And he asked, 'Well, Love. What is love?' The teacher just looked at him and told him, 'Oh, shut up and stop bullshitting me.'"

They both laughed hysterically as her sister came out of her friend's house and jumped into the back seat. The cold air that came into the car as she opened and closed the door signaled the end of this rare instant of connivance between mother and teenage daughter.

Small Talk

The younger ones had long since fallen asleep. She stepped into her room for a goodnight kiss. She had made the promise to herself that she would never go to bed without giving each and every one a good night kiss. Or at least not without trying. Despite all the will in the world, her teenagers' personal space was not always welcoming. That day turned out to be a lucky one. She sat down on her bed where a space seemed waiting for her. The mood was conducive to confidences.

"My friend Maddie has a boyfriend, you know."

"Since when?"

"It's been a few days, although they've had a thing for months."

"A thing?" They both look at each other with a hint of a smile.

"Don't tell her mom! I know you guys talk sometimes."

"Why? I'm sure she would want to know. And I am sure

she would understand."

"No, Maddie and her mom don't talk."

"That's sad, why is that?"

"Her mom works all the time; she never has time to talk."

"I'm sure she would take the time if she knew Maddie needed to share something like this. When I was working, you and I would still talk, right?"

"No, Mom, when you were working full time, we would never talk."

The sentence gutted her. She had to admit that it was true. When she lost her job of twenty years, she first felt it was like going through a divorce. But soon her mother made her realize that it was a blessing in disguise after all these years of full-time dedication, always struggling to decide who among the parents would lift the foot off the pedal when a child was sick. But it was only at that very moment that she became aware of it. So many times, she had been forced to cut short those precious moments. She would always try to read a bedtime story, of course, but would often choose the shortest possible one, knowing that she still had an email to write or a phone call with Japan once everyone was in bed. And now, there she was, fully available for her children. Was it the right state of mind, this almost state of servitude in the grip of her children? Her father once told her "Teenagers are the most ungrateful human beings." More than ever before, she knew how true that statement was. Yet, she told herself that the few years she had left before her children flew from the nest were well worth the sacrifice. She decided that although she would still engage in professional activities, necessary for their household financial equation and for her mental health, she would find a more harmonious balance for her time.

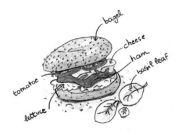

Vegetarian

That night, at the family dinner table, she stated that she had decided to become vegetarian.

"Mom, I am not asking you to change the menus, but just so you know, I will no longer eat meat."

Her dad started a diatribe about how a growing young person like her needed protein. But it wasn't a teenage crisis, nor a personal distaste for meat or a nutritional argument that had led her to that decision. She read an article indicating how cow farms were killing the planet and decided to act. This was an activist decision. A respectable one.

"Are you not going to eat foie gras and dry sausage when we go to grandpa and grandma's next summer?"

"That's going to be hard, but we'll see."

"And how about Thanksgiving, are you not going to eat turkey? I bet you won't last two months!" Continued the father.

"Stop! Can you be supportive for once?" She was now

annoyed and more determined than ever.

Weeks went by during which she hung on to her decision. Her mom had to adapt the family menus with non-meat alternatives. Within the family, the subject was understood and not much resistance was expressed as her reasons didn't emanate from an unfunded teenage attitude but from a reflected conviction. Many in the family, including the grandparents, were convinced it wouldn't last, but still they respected the commitment. A few months passed by, during which respect for her persistence grew. Some in the family even started to appreciate this lighter diet.

And then came one winter morning when the youngest woke up sick. Oh, how every parent *loves* that season, where stomach bugs and flu-like viruses overthrow well-established daily routines. It was nothing serious, but she had to stay home. Couch naps, diet and TV for a couple days. She then felt better and demanded food. Not any food, an American sandwich from the bagel place in town. Of course, like any good mother, she was overjoyed to hear her kid, who had not eaten for a few days, expressing appetite again. She ran to the place. Ordered the exact sandwich she had described. Enthused by the sweet odor of toasted bread, she ordered one for herself.

"Half sandwiches or full?"

"Full." she replied with conviction, having no idea of what she was getting herself into. After a few minutes' wait, she was given four humongous boxes within 2 large brown bags.

"There must be a mistake, I didn't order all this."

"You ordered two full American sandwiches, right?"

"Yes,"

"Then that's you."

Half ashamed, half confused, she took the bags and ran to

her car. After so many years in the United States, portions and quantities were still not her strong suit. She got home.

"The food is here."

"Mom, I haven't eaten for days, but you order as if there was an army to feed!"

"I know, he asked me if I wanted half or full sandwiches and I said full…"

The two of them painfully finished one half. An awful lot of fresh American sandwiches were left! She took a picture, texted it to her now well-established vegetarian daughter.

I know you don't eat meat, but is there anybody among your friends that would be interested in this? I know you guys have rehearsal until late. We have tons of sandwiches left-over as I ordered two full sandwiches and it turns out full is a foot long!

The response was quicker than expected:

We'll take them.

Who's 'we'?

Me.

What? There's ham in them.

Yes, I know.

But you don't eat meat?

Well, I'm very hungry.

And that sealed the end of the vegetarian era which would never be reopened. Without being fully aware of it, this imprinted the family with a long-lasting sustainability awareness. Deep inside the parents were proud of the impact their daughter had on them. That's how an individual can forge a family's whole dynamic.

Last but not Least

For the first three pregnancies in France, they stood by one fundamental principle: not to reveal anything to anyone before the twelve-week ultrasound. It was a bit out of superstition, but also there was something exhilarating in the idea of possessing such information. However, keeping the secret for three months was not without difficulty. Friends and colleagues of a young woman of childbearing age, are always on the lookout for little warning signs.

"You're not drinking coffee today?!"

"You're not drinking alcohol, eh?"

"You have a stomach bug?"

She had always been able to find a way out of the incessant sarcastic interrogations, countering adversity and unfailingly keeping the secret. Numerous times she had to rush out of the metro with an untenable urge to vomit. At work, she also had to keep track of people bathroom's whereabouts to ensure she would be there alone.

This time, circumstances would soon push her to derogate from that rule against her will. Their Italian aunt, an outstanding cook, was visiting them in New Jersey. The morning following her arrival, under the effect of the jetlag, the aunt woke up before sunrise. Not knowing what to do with herself, she went down to the kitchen, opened the fridge overflowing with food. Her cooking skills were tickled. She decided to please her hosts and started to chop and fry, unsuspecting the turmoil this would soon cause. A little trickle of grilled onion and garlic scent crept along the hallway, then along the stairs, to reach the bedrooms. In the master bedroom, it leached into the nostrils of the pregnant young women, who until that very moment was sleeping. She awoke with an irrepressible nausea. She flew down the stairs, almost tripping but determined to confront the culprit.

"Auntie, this is not going to work, you can't cook onions like that at daybreak!"

"I'm so sorry, I took the liberty to dig in your fridge, I thought I could help you by making a marinara sauce. You guys like it when I make it. It's good for pizza, for pasta. You can freeze it if you're not going to use it right away."

The secretly pregnant woman realized her earlier tone was a little aggressive. Then, in the spur of the moment, she added in a calmer tone, "I'm sorry. I'm one month pregnant and I have terrible morning sickness. All day sickness."

Auntie's face lit up and she hugged her awkwardly. She cleaned the kitchen in no time and didn't step foot in it for the rest of her stay, to the great sadness of the rest of the family. The news had leaked and flown around the world. Fortunately, baby was already holding on tight and stayed put for the next eight months.

The Little Brother

He was born in a household already occupied by five people, his parents and three sisters. Six years after the youngest of his sisters was born, his parents felt someone was missing and decided to welcome a fourth child. One last pregnancy before turning a page to move on to other chapters of parenthood and accept the aging that goes along that transition.

That was how he came to be a little boy raised by four moms, a dad... and a dog. To add a little spice, as if they lacked some and to further rebalance the male-female forces in the house, a few years after his arrival, a male dog was also adopted, a furry companion for the little brother in a way. In those years, they transitioned from a household of five to a household of seven.

When he was born, his sisters were still young. Time flew by fast and the three of them became teenagers. With that, the house was invaded with even more tears, screaming and door slamming than before, a lot of laughter too. A noisy house with four siblings, three out of four going through puberty and working parents.

For the longest time he was spared from all the conflicts. He was the cute little one that everybody loved, the one that could soothe all the pains with just a hug. He was a little angel that carried his sisters through the sorrows of life. Even when he transitioned from the cute baby brother to the annoying brother that came into his sister's room while she was Face Timing her boyfriend or reviewing for a Physics test, he always managed to get his way out with a hug and a smile. By the time he was seven, girls' mood swings were no secret to him. He also knew all about those weird tools they use in their daily lives. He knew what an eye lash curler was, what a curling iron was and, he even knew about some more intimate stuff that hangs in girls' bathrooms.

Then, as he was approaching teenage years himself, came the first stirrings of emotions for him too.

"You have a crush on Sophie!" chanted his sister giggling as she saw him abruptly end the FaceTime conversation when she opened his bedroom door.

"No, I don't."

"Yeah, yeah."

The truth was, he did have a crush on that Middle School girl even though he was still in elementary school, seduced by her charm and maturity which reminded him much more of his sisters than the dull girls his age. As was to be expected, he also experienced his first heartache when he saw her in town hand in hand with a boy. He found himself dreaming of growing up fast so that one day he could be that boy.

A Perennial Dream

It was past midnight, maybe even later in the night or closer to daybreak. Her brain, clouded by this interrupted sleep, barely conscious, registered that a tiny presence had slipped into the middle of the bed. Was he cold, did he have a nightmare? Was it just a bad habit or the need of a warm reassuring presence? Whatever the reason, the little boy slipping into their bed every night became a routine. It was trying at the time, but they would later remember it with nostalgia. Never had it happened with the three older ones who now dawdled in their own teenage universe.

"Hey, you can't be perfect on every level. It's ok," the pediatrician once said nonchalantly in reference to the issue.

And indeed, everything turned out to be fine in the end.

Maternal Guilt

First kid, the pacifier falls on the floor, you sterilize it before giving it back to your kid. Second kid, you don't sterilize it anymore, but you wash it with soap and water. Third kid, you lick it before giving it back to your child. Fourth kid and beyond, if by misfortune a pacifier falls on the ground or ends up in the dog's mouth, they will just get it themselves and put it back in their mouth as it is.

Somebody had told her that story a long time ago. It could be interpreted in many ways. Some would affirm younger ones tend to be the most resourceful and independent. Others admit that younger ones may be the most neglected. She liked to think that having siblings would teach her kids to be self-sufficient while knowing they could count on unconditional friends. In her idyllic vision, she had no doubt she could always find a way to be in multiple places at once. She learned the hard way that even if she loved each and every one with all her heart, her attention wasn't infallible. The level of care was not proportional to the rank among the siblings, rather a consequence of how many pots were on the stove at the same time.

One day, the phone rang while she was still with her client. It was the mother of her youngest daughter's friend. The girls were running in the park and she had tripped. Her wrist was bruised and swollen. The benevolent mother had applied ice and a bandage. Everything was fine now. Her workday was almost over. She wrapped up a few things and jumped into her car. She couldn't help but feel guilty for not being there to console her injured daughter right away. She felt as if her hectic life was flowing like a high-speed train. She picked up her daughter after profusely thanking the other mother, who, unlike her, had been there for the incident.

A couple days passed during which her daughter continued to complain of pain in her wrist. The schedule was so packed that she convinced herself and her daughter that it was nothing and that it would soon pass. In case any of this was just a need for attention, she hugged her and told her she loved her. How many times had she rushed to the emergency room for a simple sprain? It was nothing serious. By the third day, the wrist had doubled in size, she couldn't bend it and the persisting bluish color was turning into a blackish purple. Guilt seized her again. Was she ignoring something serious? She called the school, work and drove her kid to the urgent care. Her daughter was taken to the x-ray room. The radiologist set her up in the control room from where she was able to see all the pictures that were taken of her daughter's wrist. She heard the operator murmur "Yeah, it's broken, double fracture without a doubt." At that moment, all the guilt that was dormant in her burst. A few tears came to her eyes. She remembered her friend telling her the story of her daughter who woke up every night. She would hug her and tell her that she loved her very much. It turned out that the little one had a cyclic ear infection. She could care less about her mother's kisses, her ears just hurt. Likewise, her little one was broken and in pain and she had been blind to it.

When brought back to the waiting room, her daughter inquired, "Is it broken? Do you know?"

"I'm not sure," the mother mumbled, "It might be."

She knew full well that there was a double fracture. As if with her nuanced response she was trying to hide the deep shame of ignoring the cues her daughter had been sending her. The doctor, as expected, confirmed the fracture. A beautiful sky-blue cast was placed around her wrist and arm.

"She is young, so the bones should be like new in three weeks and all this will be ancient history!" he added with a big smile, used to these little obstacles in children's life. "I will write a note for gym exemption. You are a righty, correct? Shouldn't bother you too much for school otherwise."

"Yes!" She admitted with a smile that couldn't hide the joy at being exempt from the gym for several weeks.

As they were walking back to the car her daughter inquired "When I asked you, you knew it was broken, right?"

To which the remorseful mother answered, "You're right, I heard the guy say it. I'm sorry I didn't listen to you when you said you were in pain. Part of me wanted to spare you, which was silly. It would just delay the news a few minutes."

"I told you so! But it's ok mom, don't worry, I love you. I can't wait to have my friends sign my cast; this is going to be fun. They're all going to be like, wait, what happened to you?!"

And this is how the guilt of the mother was cleared off by

the candor and the total absence of resentment from her child. She was now immersed in her own world where this unfortunate trivial event became a source of novelty and excitement.

"Wait, I can't play the flute either!" She exclaimed all smiles. "No band! This is awesome!"

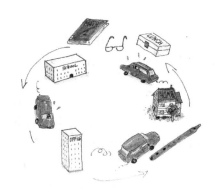

Maternal Servitude

Phone calls and texts came every day.

"Hi, I'm calling from the school's office, everything is fine, but your daughter forgot her glasses and she is complaining she can't see the white board. Any chance you could drop them off?"

"Hi, it's the school principal. Everything is fine, but your child doesn't have a lunch; she says she left her lunch box in the back seat of the car. Is there any way you could still drop it off?"

The older ones would summon their mother by text without the slightest shame as well.

Help, left my essay on the printer, I'm going to get a zero.

Sometimes the threat even included financial consequences that ironically the mother would have to undertake.

Mom, it's the last day to bring back my chemistry

textbook or we'll have to pay $25. The use of the pro-
noun 'we' irritated her even though she knew full well that the
money would come out of her pocket.

Working now independently, she had more freedom than
when she was tied to the corporate world, yet how many times
had she made a detour on her way to her client or skipped her
lunch to drop off food, books, signed forms, instruments, play
scripts, gym bags, or pads sealed in a brown bag? Until the
day she had an epiphany. The servitude into which she had
sunk jumped in her face and she decided to free herself forever. That day, she had given up her lunch so she could drop
a flute at the school's main office. She rang the school bell. An
amiable voice through the speaker inquired on what she was
dropping off.

"My daughter's flute." She responded.

"I'm sorry, mam, school policy has changed and we are
not accepting instrument drop offs. Music teachers want students to assume responsibility for their instruments."

With these words she returned to her car, a little vexed and
ashamed, but swearing she would never give in again. She was
forced to recognize the school was shaking her softness, slap-
ping her 'snowplow parenting' and putting her back on a right
track. After that day, oddly enough, forgotten objects became
increasingly rare. The phone calls and the text buzzes dwin-
dled as well. The children adopted strategies other than crying
for help to their mother. More sharing of food with friends,
exchanges of locker codes, borrowing of sneakers took place.
She never admitted it but deep inside, although she was happy
to see her children grow and gain autonomy, she couldn't help
but miss the feeling of being indispensable.

Ward Off the Evil

After an early morning appointment at the dentist, she dropped her daughter off in front of school a little later than usual. School was already in session. She watched her walk away. As always, her daughter had connected her phone into the car Bluetooth. She would always do that, even if the ride was a few minutes long. It was unimaginable not to take advantage of even a couple minutes to assume the role of family DJ for the shortest party in history. Besides, basic radio was not worthy of her time. So, as the teenager walked away from the car, the music coming from her phone started to crackle and break before disconnecting from the Bluetooth. The mother watched her ring the doorbell and enter the mysterious and trying lair that was the high school. Her thoughts took a dark turn. She caught herself being afraid and longing for one thing: to fast-forward the rest of the day. That way, the evening would come, all the family members would be safe and gathered again at home for dinner, after an uneventful but no less enriching day. No doubt there would be screams and arguments, but everyone would be back to their safe base after a long free-spirited day playing tag in the wild. Sometimes it was random news items, that she couldn't help but read or listen to, that would ignite her anxiety: school shootings, road accidents, overdoses, suicides. Misfortune had also stroke at the very heart of her community, striking some little more than children. During those devastating times, it was as if the wolf, whose image once kept her daughter from sleeping, was roaming and assailing. Her strong belief that an auspicious star was looking after them was undermined. But she had her own way, dictated by a self-preservation instinct, to ward off maleficent spirits that would try to slip through the cracks of her shield.

Influential Educators

It was the night before her daughter's audition. They were driving home when the teenager burst into tears. In an attempt to find the right maternal words, she insisted everything would be fine, but the teenager wasn't listening, nothing her mother could say could calm her down.

"My throat hurts, I can't sing," she whispered in between sniffles.

"I'll make you a tea with honey. I also have these miraculous cough drops; it's going to be fine."

"Shut up, you don't know what you're talking about," she interjected.

"Excuse me? Did I just hear 'shut up'?"

"I'm sorry, I'm sorry. I didn't mean it. But seriously leave me alone."

"Ok, just trying to help here." The tone of the conversation which could have gone down a very ugly path, calmed down. "Should we call your voice teacher? Maybe she has some tips on what to do to help with your throat?" she added, feeling an external mediator could maybe solve the imbroglio.

"Ok."

"Should we call now?"

"Yeah."

A little surprised by the ease with which her daughter had accepted, she handed her the phone so she could dial herself, as the phone was on Bluetooth.

"I'll let you do the talking. Pretend I'm not here," she instructed.

The conversation was quick. The teacher's tone was comforting but firm. She didn't sink into commiseration, but on the contrary summoned her to pull herself together.

"Some people, like me, do this for a living, you know. Whether your throat hurts or not, you just can't dwell on the hurdles. You grab the bull by the horns." She recommended to get a small vaporizer, an infusion with honey, a good night's sleep and ensured her everything would be fine. After the straightforward pep talk, the young girl came around, the attitude had switched, the mindset was now combative and determined. After witnessing the effect that this external human being had had on her daughter, she was forced to admit that certain situations had to be handled by someone other than the parents.

It was not the first time this had happened. Year after year, life had forced her to shake off a certain do-it-all feeling. Teaching their kids how to bike, swim, ski, even drive—freakiest of all, considering it had to happen during the most confrontational years—always occurred in the midst of painful parent-child quarrels, but in absolute serenity when handled by another adult, whether a grandparent or a young and good-looking instructor.

Even years after her eldest started school for the first time and she realized she was grasping knowledge from sources outside her household, she couldn't help but being amazed at the influence certain teachers could have. As life went by, she learned to delegate whole sections of the children's education to others with trust and to even use that power in her favor: "If you don't sleep in your bed, I will tell your teacher tomorrow that you are a baby." She wasn't proud at the cheap shot, but the threat would be terrifying enough for the kids to comply. The relationships forged with some influential teachers had lasting effects for life. She knew it from experience. All her life she had been driven by this adage from a philosophy professor during her senior year back in France: "Why are you stressed? What is at stake? Always assess what is at stake before even sinking into stress mode, because most of the time you will realize how inconsequential it is," he would assert. When she worked in a corporate environment, on the brink of high-level meetings, she would tell herself, "What is at stake? It's only shampoo, not heart surgery," and pursue with alleviated anxiety.

In their family, anecdotes of certain teachers would enliven conversations at the dinner table and remain engraved in memories, especially of those whose classes had been experienced by several of the siblings. The whole family cherished the memory of that particular teacher who claimed to have "grading elves" at home. These were lazy at times, which would delay the students getting their grades back. The same teacher had compared without flinching the epic of Ulysses to Dory's voyage (the unconditional friend of Nemo in Disney's animated movies), which, with young adults of sixteen or seventeen years-old had led to very mixed reactions. There was also this Biology teacher, so oblivious to what was happening in class, that girls would do their nails without her ever noticing.

Some teachers were made fun of, in fair game. Others were feared. And then, some were worshipped or even crystallized youthful crushes. All, in the end, forged the character of youth in one way or another.

"My English teacher is so bad, Mom, he's not worth the taxes you guys pay," she said in a tone so mature that her parents were floored. "You never had such bad teachers during your freshman year," she continued, addressing now her big sister.

"What are you talking about? I did too. Remember my 9th grade Biology teacher? But all you need from them is a good grade. And if their class sucks, oh well, you're wasting your time a bit, but you get a good grade and that's what matters."

"But I am so mad, I used to like English. He's ruined it for me."

Her older sister shrugged her shoulders in response.

A few years later, the most opinionated and outspoken of both sisters came back home furious and somehow resigned.

"I got a zero in English."

"Why? What happened?"

"I didn't turn in my essay."

"Why?" Replied the whole family choir in unison, shocked in face of such unprecedented situation.

"I hate the book; I can't write an essay on a book I hate. I told him and he said I have the right not to like the book, but I would get a zero for not turning in my essay."

"There isn't much to argue against that," replied the

father. "What book is it that you hate so much?"

"The Scarlet Letter. It's so depressing and boring and ancient. And sexist. I just can't. I mean, I read the book, which was already a lot!"

"But you cannot just decide you are not doing the work and expect not to get a zero," her rational sister added.

"I know."

The educator's ultimate lesson had been learned. Anyone is entitled to defend what they believe in but must be ready to assume the consequences, whatever they may be.

Track My Teenager

"We're going pumpkin picking tomorrow!" declared the parents with enthusiasm seeking to stir up the crowds.

"Cool, I can take pictures and maybe there will be a good one I can post," replied the youngest, who had just been given the privilege of a cell phone and entered the world of social media.

"We're not going just for you to hunt down a picture you can post. We're going to enjoy a nice family outing," replied the father.

Since their daughter had been granted access to social media, her life had sort of become a succession of events that had to be shared on the public platforms for all to see. It was as if moments in life were only of value if they could be posted. A post was not to be uploaded at random times. Each day was punctuated by narrow windows of opportunity that would guarantee an optimal number of likes, which, in turn, would forge "popularity."

Determining timely access to a cell phone and thereby opening the possibility for their teen to dive without a safety net into the terrifying universe of social media was not the most dreadful of all parental dilemmas. Entrusting their teen with a phone also meant affixing a GPS device on them. Was it better to lose sleep out of concern for what your teens are doing while being able to track their location or not? For the longest time she wondered why any loving parent wouldn't take advantage of technology to follow their adolescent movements, until a certain event triggered a mind shift in that respect.

It was past midnight and it had been two hours since she had last heard from her daughter who had initially left with the intention of going to two parties, one after the other. Concern was mounting in her mind. She examined her husband for a few seconds. He was asleep and blissfully snoring. How could he be so carefree? Her anguish, mixed with a touch of anger, made her want to wake him up. But she ended up reasoning herself. She decided to use the last resort instead, tracking her daughter's phone. Plunging into her child's life and privacy, she saw the small green dot which represented her daughter in the middle of a random street, north of their city. The green dot was there, active, as the app would specify, sharp and standstill. Sometimes the location was approximate in which case the app would locate the phone within a wide grey circle. But in this case, there was no doubt, the phone was lying in the middle of a random street. She felt her heart rate speeding, her blood boiling, tears rising. The simplest and most logical explanation—she could have dropped her phone—gave way to the most dreadful theories. Her daughter had been kidnapped, had been hit by a car or worse. The scenarios her mind was making up were worsening by the minute. The powerlessness that invaded her acted as a catalyst in a chain reaction, fueling an irrepressible and exponentially growing anguish. Immersed in a state of mental block, she had no idea how much time had passed when she heard a commotion on her driveway. It could have been just a few minutes or several hours. She couldn't tell. But at that moment, she was convinced that someone was coming to share a terrible news. She tumbled down the stairs. Someone was trying to open the side kitchen door. Through the small window, she saw her daughter, more than tipsy. A tall boy, visibly sober, was holding her. Despite the darkness, she recognized him, he was her best friend's boyfriend.

"Hi, Ma'am, she is not feeling very well. I'm very sorry, but she's home safe now," he seemed relieved, but uncomfortable.

"It's ok, thank you so much for taking care of her and bringing her home."

The mother closed the door and felt all the adrenaline that had invaded her fade and make room to exhaustion.

"Honey, where is your phone?"

The young lady had no idea, nor did she have any recollection of the events of that night. Now was not the time to reprimand; the conversation would have to take place in the sobriety of the following day. As she was tucking the drowsy young lady in bed, the computer started ringing. It was one of her daughter's friends calling on FaceTime. The mother clicked on the green button.

"She's home, don't worry and thank you for your concern. We are all good. She lost her phone somehow. Seems it's somewhere it in the middle of Lawrence Avenue."

"I think that might be in front of my house; do you want me to try and find it?" replied the young person on the other end of the line.

"It's late, I don't want you to go out."

"I don't mind, give me a few minutes, just make it ring."

A few minutes went by, through the tracking app, the mother clicked on 'play sound'.

"I think I hear it," said the hopeful voice. "Do you mind staying on the line with me? There's a group of sketchy kids passing by... I got it! Should I bring it to you now?"

"No, please go home, she can live for a day at least without her phone! We will touch base tomorrow to pick it up."

"Ok, good night!"

"Good night, thank you very much for your help, you guys are such good friends."

After all these unexpected undertakings, the night was short, but everyone slept soundly. The young lady's hangover the next day served as a wakeup call. This wouldn't be her last boozy night, but at least for the following ones, she was well aware of the consequences. Parents could only hope for smarter choices. As for the mother, she used the phone tracker much more sparingly. Letting go and trusting took time. Although she never managed to relax and sleep as her husband, progress was made.

Existential Contradiction

Time flies, they say. As time goes by, it seems as if everything moves a little faster every day. As parents caught in this incessant whirlwind, they had to handle an insurmountable internal conflict: the deep desire to freeze time to enjoy the moment indefinitely and the consuming impatience to discover the adults that their children would become.

All her life she had made sure to write down in a notebook those moments in life that seemed important. But it was at this point in her life that she began to build the idea of doing something with them.

Send-off

Everlasting Reminiscences - 2018 and Hereafter

"It's all a great mystery… Look up at the sky and you'll see how everything changes"

Antoine de Saint-Exupéry – Le Petit Prince

Road Trip

Very early on, he was determined to be a pioneer in the world of electric cars and clean energy. Their undisputable outstanding safety features and cleaner technology became a no-brainer. Even hybrid options were no longer up to par. He shifted the numbers in the family budget, made some cuts elsewhere and managed to convince her to switch not only one of their gas cars to electric, but both. Thereby, they became an all-electric family, intriguing their neighbors and friends.

"How far can you travel? How many miles does the charge handle? How long does it take to charge?"

A living advertisement for Elon Musk, which also implied occasional embarrassment for the kids, especially the teenagers as they had to emerge from under the falcon wing doors when being dropped at school; but it would soon become the norm. It is interesting to note that for the youngest, who barely knew how to speak, there was no cause for shame or even curiosity in driving an electric car equipped with an auto-pilot software.

After acquiring their family size electric SUV, they decided to undertake a thousand miles road trip from New Jersey to Orlando, first among the many that they would accomplish over the years to follow. Taking a family of six on such an adventure was not without risks and they often feared that they would kill each other along the way. These trips proved to be a strong foundation for strengthening their family ties, in the same way their journey through Europe had been years before that. Forced to share teen love sorrows, agree on the same music or audiobooks, synchronize bathroom and food breaks... Memorable laughter would seal forever their bonds, like when a battle to get rid of a humongous mosquito some-where in South Carolina ended up in it being smashed on the fancy white ceiling, staining it forever in red. There was screaming in all directions.

"Open the windows!"

"Noooo, close the windows, we have the AC on!"

"Don't smash it, it's going to stain!"

"It's going to bite us!"

"Ahhhh..."

"Take a wet cloth now!"

"Soak the blood before it dries!"

Everything had led to that one moment. No more tears because of a recent teenage break up, no more stress because of a work email... Nothing else but big, united laughter. It may have only lasted a few minutes, but it would be remem-bered for a lifetime.

World Cup

The empty bottle of Don Perignon was there in the middle of the counter, like a vestige from the past. The bottle encapsulated laughter, shouting and happy moments. Coming closer to it, one could almost still hear:

"Gooooooal !!!!!"

"Come oooon!"

"Did he get hurt or is he faking it?"

All those lines, so familiar and mundane around a soccer game. It was a bit like listening to the breeze through the interstices of a seashell. A real illusion. July 15th, 2018 was far away, yet seemed like yesterday. That day, the house had been full for the occasion. France didn't make it to the World Cup final every day. It hadn't happened in twenty years! More frequent than most comets, but in a way just as fleeting. Two different audiences had besieged different rooms. Adults in the living room, young people in the family room. Some young adults had decided to team up with the grown-ups. It was there that the Don Perignon was flowing. The adults were a little upset because a tiny lag in the sound gave a few seconds' advantage to the younger group watching the soccer game in the family room. In the living room, the suspense of each goal was spoiled by bursts of excitement coming from that other room, always a few seconds before the action. Regardless, the celebration was nonetheless memorable. France won 4-2 against Croatia. An exultation that brought back the immense joy from 1998 when France beat Brazil 3-0. Everyone embraced and congratulated each other until the last drop of champagne. At the end of the day, once everything had been put away and cleaned, the eldest saved the empty bottle in extremis from being tossed, as if she had sensed a genius of memories had been caught in it that could emerge years later and grant the wish of an impalpable flashback.

Letting Go

To move their first born to college, they undertook a long and painful family road trip. The Tesla was packed. All the family members were squeezed like sardines in between boxes, bags, baskets of disparate shapes, a coffee maker, a mini vacuum cleaner and heterogeneous objects wedged in unused tiny spaces and ready to fall as soon as the trunk would be opened. After a very brief spark of excitement at the prospect of this adventure, throughout the entire trip, the youngest two kept asking themselves why they had been forced to be part of the ordeal. The oldest spent her time longing for her freedom finally within arm's reach. The second one, who was next in line to fly off to college a couple years after, indicated to her parents that for her it would be out of the question for the whole family to come. The separation and the last big family hug were tearful, nonetheless. Bad moods and arguments had been forgotten at that point. The big sister was leaving the nest. Reality took shape at that precise moment.

A few years later, she said goodbye to her second child on the porch of the house. Her father was going to drive her. As the car was pulling away, an unexpected memory slipped into her thoughts. The beautiful and tall young woman taking off that day, had been three years old once; it felt as if it were yesterday. She remembered being at the pediatrician's, in the waiting room, when the determined little girl had taken off her diaper and decreed, "I am a big girl now; I no longer need a diaper."

She had been strong-willed like that since a very young age. As a mom, she remembered doubting at that very moment her ability to behave like the big girl she claimed to be, to realize quickly enough, she was already a woman of her word. Now she was watching her go and was forced to admit that another page was turning. She knew that in the blink of an eye the other two would be gone too, each towards their unique life project.

That night, she went to bed with both a sense of accomplishment and the feeling of having aged a little.

The days, weeks, months that followed were punctuated by FaceTime calls for which she always had time, any time of the day or night.

"I have a headache, what do I take?"

"My throat hurts."

"How often do I wash my bed sheets?"

"Can I put my leggings in the dryer?"

"Can I put bread in the microwave?"

Later on, living in an off-campus apartment:

"The chicken I bought is two days expired, can I still cook it?"

"What do I use to clean the mold in the shower?"

After all, the umbilical cord was never cut abruptly and it felt good that way for everyone.

Flying with their Own Wings

Referring to his elder sister, the youngest inquired, "When she finishes college, will she still be living at home with us?

"I don't think so."

"But where will she live then?"

"She will have her own home."

"But where?"

"Wherever she finds a job."

"Can we still visit her?"

"Of course, and she will visit us as well. Maybe if she doesn't live too far, like in the city for example and you are old enough, you can visit her on your own."

"Really?"

"Why not? Someday you will be old enough to take the train by yourself."

"But Mom…"

"Yes?"

"Can I live with you and dad forever?"

Hair Gel

The house, once filled with screams, had become quieter. It had also become predominantly male, which was unheard of. The young boy had his nose buried in his bowl of cereal and his eyes locked on his tablet streaming the latest Pokémon episode for the umpteenth time, when his father walked up to him with the jar of hair gel in his hand.

"How do you do this again?" he asked. His son barely looked up.

"Dad, I have explained hundreds of times already. You take a dime-sized amount with your fingertip; you rub it in your hands and then apply into your hair the same way you do with shampoo." He paused for a few seconds, distracted by a huge explosion on the screen. "Then you shape your hair into the style you want. You can use a comb if you want," he added. "Come to the bathroom, I'll show you one more time." He had learned by watching a video on YouTube and now was passing the baton to his father.

For a few minutes uncontrollable laughter arose from the bathroom where father and son experimented hairstyles, each one crazier than the next.

The son emerged with a mohawk, the dad with a sober style more suitable for his working day.

While his father's authority remained unchallenged on subjects such as math or astrophysics, for a few more years still, his son was teaching him how to remain a cool, trendy dad. What's more, having grown up so attuned to women, it was often he who gave his dad the best gift ideas for his mom or sisters.

Family Tree House

Mother's Day and Father's Day had both always been pinned on multiple dates on the kitchen calendar. For whatever reason, dates to honor parents vary by country and their family tree was made of members scattered around the planet. By implicit agreement, the greatest festivities were always planned on the date of the place where they were. The other dates were an occasion for diverse celebrations, including phone calls to grandmothers and aunts around the world, flower or sweet treat deliveries. Whatever the circumstances, in their family, it was a not-to-be-missed moment of the year, the cornerstone of their clan.

That morning the house was still snoozing, in sync with the old dog snoring on the living room rug. The children were now all gone, one after the other without anybody realizing it. Some of them were still coming and going, carrying and storing armloads of possessions and dirty laundry. The eight small trees that she had once carried in her trunk and planted when the youngest was born had become giant pines. When she looked at them, sometimes she wondered how it had been possible for all of them to fit in her trunk, yet she knew they had been that small once. After the last one left the nest, they decided on some home improvements, never interfering with their personal spaces. Bedroom walls were still covered with pictures and memories of their school years, smiles and friends long gone on the adventure of life, books read in their youth, both those reluctantly read for school or joyfully when chosen freely.

Everyone would be arriving soon. The freezer had been loaded with ice pops and the kitchen cabinets with chocolate cookies, the same ones they had cherished in their childhood.

And so, everyone landed, travelling from their various horizons, some far away, some less distant. The house woke up to laughter and hugs. The usual order in the absence of the children was shaken. Bags, shoes, jackets and toys tossed all over the floor, chairs and couches, signaled the consented colonization of the beloved home-base. In a flash, conversations started and intermingled.

"How's your internship in the new unit going?"

"It's hard; I don't get any sleep, I'm mostly doing night shifts, but I'm liking it, I'm learning a lot."

The biggest sister, now a young mother also expecting a second one, burst into the conversation between her younger sister and her mother.

"Do you have a cookie that I can give him?"

"But dinner will be ready very soon."

"He's cranky."

"It's funny, I remember when you would prohibit cookies

for your brother if we were too close to dinner!"

"Now I get why you would sometimes give up, Mom."

"Do you still have morning sickness?"

"Yah, I still do."

"Poor thing, they've lasted way more than three months. Must be genetics, I was like that with you."

"I know, but now I manage them better, as long as I eat enough."

"Mom…"

"Yeah?"

"I'm scared I won't know what to do."

"You will know what to do, better than anybody else. Just follow your instinct. If you have doubts, choose one person. It can be me, a friend, a neighbor, but only one and that's the person you listen to." As she was saying that to her daughter, a deluge of memories poured into her mind.

"How did you do it, when we were all little?"

"It was an adventure, sleep deprivation and temperatures. Later on, being punched and yelled at!" She declared pointedly with a touch of humor. "But all in all, we had fun, we still do and I suspect you will too."

Meanwhile, the family room and the backyard shack opened up to a second life. From the treasure chests burst a profusion of toys that had been laying in hibernation. Some still emitted sounds which to the ears of the young parents awakened the memories of a colorful childhood.

The day unfolded with music, singing and a few old-time board games, but not without some vigorous debates between siblings or robust discussions between parents and their now adult offspring. They were more likeminded than they would admit, despite their tenacious souls.

At some point, the mother was alone with her four children, while the rest of the crowd was playing outside.

"Guys, we need to talk about dad's birthday, it's a big one this year," she said.

"We have been discussing it over our group chat, it's all planned," responded the oldest.

"What group chat? I haven't seen anything," inquired the mother.

"I'm talking about *our* group chat."

"You guys have your own group chat?" she was clearly a little vexed.

"You bet we do, we've had it for years, since way before I left for college!"

Of course, they had a siblings' group chat. Part of her knew that, but somehow the fact sunk in. She didn't conceptualize why, but the idea made her proud and fulfilled. She felt as if no matter what, the four of them would always be there for each other.

After dark, while everyone was gone, the youngest of the sisters was wandering around the house. She was staying over until the next day. She could hear her mother whistling while preparing a light pasta broth for the late dinner. Her father was beginning to doze in the living room, as was the old pooch and pretty much everything between these walls full of stories and happy laughing ghosts. She could hear "Did you finish your homework?" "Can you please set up the table?" "Could you two just stop fighting?" "You're grounded, no more screens for two days!" "It's so unfair, why does she get away with this?" "I'm always the forgotten one." "Can you get out of my room?" "She stole my sweater!" She could hear the loud music and the melodies. "I love you to the moon and back."

"I'm so proud of you." As she was sinking into her thoughts, somewhat bewitched by these imaginary voices and sounds, she saw a stack of paper on a corner of the family desk. It looked like a manuscript. She got closer, ran her fingers over it with a slight and fleeting touch and read the header *Family memories – For my beloved children*. She browsed through it.

Towards the end, she uncovered a story about a road trip across America. A couple taking advantage of their new freedom. Then there was this new *pied à terre* in Canada. She turned around and saw her mother.

"Mom, are you and dad planning on going on a road trip?"

"Yes, we have been planning this for a long time."

"How about this house in Canada?"

"We are going to put our house on the market and we will see where the wind takes us."

The young woman's eyes were now full of tears. She felt immensely happy for her parents to continue their globe-trotting adventures.

Epilogue

"One sees clearly only with the heart. Anything essential is
invisible to the eyes"

Antoine de Saint-Exupéry – Le Petit Prince

He was an old soul. He had been part of the family for more years than he could count. They adopted him when he was about twelve weeks. What had happened before that was blurry. His love for them had been instantaneous and remained unconditional. He quickly became the lead of the pack. None of them ever realized it, but he was. His mission in life was to protect them, especially the youngest one. For some reason, he cared for him more than for anyone else. Maybe because they grew up together. Or maybe because he sensed that he was often the center of everybody's attention, both the sisters and the dad and the mom. He knew the mother believed she was the lead. But she wasn't. She was his master. She fed him, walked him, threw him his ball. He hated when she would give him a bath, but he would subdue. For those things she had the final say. Sometimes, and that's what made him the happiest, she would hug him or scratch his belly, they all did. But he was the lead of the family. And that is why when they walked him around, he had to walk ahead. He did sense that they were always annoyed at the fact that, even in his older days, he had never stopped pulling the leash so he could walk in front of everyone. He had to fulfill his duty: to shield them. He knew that some of them had given up walking him because of that. When they spoke, their voices were always switching from one tone to another. He got used to it when he was young. Sometimes they meant the same thing, but they used different sounds. Maybe he had it in his genes. He was a Catahoula Leopard; his ancestors were a mix between American and European dogs. No doubt fate brought him to this family. Some of the visitors they had would speak in a flatter, less tuneful manner. They seemed to come from far, carrying lots of unfamiliar smells. They stayed for a while, some of them walked him. Then, they would always leave at some point. He missed them when they were not there. Sometimes there was a commotion; He heard their voices, everyone gathered in the living room for a while and seemed very happy, but he couldn't smell their presence. It was very peculiar. Some of them would show up again, he would recognize their familiar scents. All this made him smarter than his fellows at the park. He had been through it all with them. Always feeling their joys and their sorrows, hearing their arguments and their celebrations. His universe was loud and musical. When they were away for a long time, he was sad and thought of nothing but the fact that he was waiting for them. His pack was a very tight one, though, and he knew they were always coming back to this place that he called home.

Acknowledgments

My unending gratitude goes to:

My fellow writers from the Westfield NJ "Shut up and Write" group. This collection of stories would never have seen the light of day without their support and encouragement. During the pandemic, we stuck together in a way that will unite us forever.

Tom Jenks and my fellow writers from "The Art of the Story" workshop. Our regular gatherings keep me enlightened, challenged and energized in a truly transformative way.

Apprentice House Press for trusting me. As a first-time author, I couldn't dream of a more collaborative, kind-hearted and professional process.

My family, they are the cornerstone of my life and my source of inspiration. They believed in me from the outset, they are the ones who push me forward.

About the Author

Cecilia Y. Saint-Denis lives in the United States, in Westfield, New Jersey with her family. After working for 20 years in the consumer goods industry, she decided to immerse herself in the adventure of writing and give herself the time and space to put these stories jostling in her head into words. Having been an avid reader her entire life and being the parent of four children now 10 to 22 years old, she has always been particularly touched by stories that reflect on parenthood, childhood, adolescence, and coming of age struggles. Her favorite genre: short stories and narrative non-fiction; her preferred themes: all matters relating to family and relationships. The stories that she is offering us reflect on these very subjects. They are rooted in personal experiences to then take off with a touch of poetry.

About the Illustrator

Stéphanie Weppelmann is a French artist, currently living in Leipzig Germany. She has a background in art history and graphic design, that she studied in Paris and Italy. She teaches art to both children and adults. She has always seen the art of illustration as a mean to express ideas and feelings in a powerful way. She finds inspiration during her walks, trips, museums tours, and thorough observation of plants, animals, and people. She sees humor as a crucial component in her illustrations. When Cecilia approached her asking her to give life to her stories, she was immediately enthusiastic, having grown up reading the delightfully illustrated stories of Le Petit Nicolas. She found immediate inspiration in Cecilia's text that felt touching, sensitive, and relatable to her, also a dedicated mother of two sons.

Apprentice
House Press
Loyola University Maryland

Apprentice House is the country's only campus-based, student-staffed book publishing company. Directed by professors and industry professionals, it is a nonprofit activity of the Communication Department at Loyola University Maryland.

Using state-of-the-art technology and an experiential learning model of education, Apprentice House publishes books in untraditional ways. This dual responsibility as publishers and educators creates an unprecedented collaborative environment among faculty and students, while teaching tomorrow's editors, designers, and marketers.

Eclectic and provocative, Apprentice House titles intend to entertain as well as spark dialogue on a variety of topics. Financial contributions to sustain the press's work are welcomed. Contributions are tax deductible to the fullest extent allowed by the IRS.

To learn more about Apprentice House books or to obtain submission guidelines, please visit www.apprenticehouse.com.

Apprentice House
Communication Department
Loyola University Maryland
4501 N. Charles Street
Baltimore, MD 21210
410-617-5265
info@apprenticehouse.com • www.apprenticehouse.com